SPITTING IMAGE

HARMONY REED

STERLING & STONE

SPITTING IMAGE

Chapter One

THE SONG WAS ALMOST OVER.

"Fake Plastic Trees" by Radiohead. Everett just wanted to hear the last verse. He could circle the block one more time. Ever since he'd gotten the call, he'd been numb, his chest so frozen that he could barely breathe. His adoptive brothers, Marco and Roberto, had done nothing to soften the blow — in fact, Everett was sure they'd relished the opportunity to drop the news on him like it was nothing before hanging up.

Mom's dead. Funeral's tomorrow. Show up or don't, we don't care.

How was he supposed to tell Clara when he didn't believe it himself?

How could he explain to his son that Grandma was gone?

He hadn't even known she was sick.

No way could he take Jimi to the funeral, not when his brothers had made it clear that Everett was unwelcome. He'd done everything he could to keep his son away from the bullies who were, unfortunately, his foster brothers.

Worse, Clara would understand, but she wouldn't *understand*. She expected Everett to stick to the schedule no matter what came up, even if the emergency wasn't his fault.

He was a grown man, dammit. He shouldn't be scared of his ex-wife. He wasn't, really. It just made him sick to his stomach knowing that no matter what choice he made, Clara was going to have a problem with it.

He needed something to soften her up … an opening line that might help them start out with a little reset on some of their most recent bullshit, maybe remind her in a quiet way of what they'd once shared. What they could still share … in a new way, if she was ever willing to allow it. They had a child together, they could do better than "make the best of it."

Now that Mom was gone, that seemed more important than ever. But when was the last time they'd talked without fighting?

Maybe he should start with a compliment about whatever she was wearing. Clara took a lot of her pride in her personal aesthetic, and that was something Everett had always truly appreciated about her.

Wow! I really love that dress! Is it a Jubilee?

Her favorite dresses came from Jubilee. Even if the one she was wearing didn't, the reference might make her smile. *Am I allowed to tell you how great you look in that dress?*

One more time around the block. He started the song again.

The car was still quiet, and his thoughts turned even more depressing.

Six days until his birthday. That meant his birthday week had officially started: the most special week of any year for Everett. Usually the *only* special week.

But from this point on, he was going to remember it as the anniversary of the worst day of his life.

He pulled over to check his phone.

No messages from Marco and Roberto, asking how Mom could have deteriorated so quickly.

His best friends, the Ds, were radio silent as well.

And still nothing from Gavin Cash, the private investigator that he'd hired a couple weeks ago to find his biological family.

His brothers' lack of communication wasn't surprising. The Ds were probably busy with their own families. But waiting to hear back from Cash was killing him.

Enough stalling.

One more deep breath, then Everett was out of the car and up on the porch, ringing the doorbell, still deciding exactly how to best compliment Clara's dress.

She answered wearing a loose blouse and slim-fitting jeans. "You're here. Finally."

"You said 7ish."

"Is this what *ish* means to you?"

"I'm super sorry—"

"I hope you're 'super apologizing' for Jimi being the last one in class to get his emergency bag and donations turned in. At this point, 'sorry for being late' is a given."

Everett looked down, but only for a moment so he could bear to look back up at her.

"Holy shit, Clara. I totally-double forgot about that. I know I told you like eleventy-hundred times that I had it, and I really, really did. I even bought all the stuff. It's in the stockroom at Joe's. I can—"

"Shove it up your ass, Everett. That's what you can do." Clara sighed. "You fucking exhaust me. And I know I just swore at you twice and I'm sorry for that. But I took care of it. Miss Bradshaw called me because Jimi was crying. I'm sick of—"

"I know. I'm sorry. You're totally right."

"You can't just keep telling me I'm right without ever doing anything to change your behavior, Ev. You have an example to set for your son."

His throat constricted in pain, but he forced himself to speak anyway. "Something happened."

"What?" Clara eyed him, suspiciously. "You're shutting down Java Joe's?"

"No! I'm not—" Could she not just give him a break this once, when he was obviously too broken up to think straight? "About this weekend—"

"No way. You are *not* weaseling out of taking your son again—"

"I'm not weaseling out of anything! I have to go to my mom's funeral."

That surprised her. "I'm sorry for your loss, Everett, I really am. But …"

"But?"

"But that doesn't change the fact that you agreed to take Jimi this weekend."

Was she deaf? What could she have planned for this weekend that was more important than his mother's funeral? Was he not allowed a single day to honor her memory?

"I'm not planning a trip to Vegas, Clara. *It's my mother's funeral.*"

"You're always doing this to us."

"I'm not doing anything to you. I have no control over when my mother dies."

"You're right, Everett. Rationally, of course I get it. And maybe I wouldn't be ready to claw your fucking eyeballs out right now if you hadn't done this to me,

4

and more importantly to Jimi, a hundred times before."

"The restaurant has been busy," he lied.

"It's not a restaurant, and it's only busy if *busy* is a synonym for *bullshit*."

"You're not being fair."

"I have gigs all weekend — which is how I earn a living to support our child, something that wouldn't be as urgent if you were keeping up with your child support."

Everett stifled his anger that she'd brought up the issue of money yet again. "I can take Jimi next weekend if you can switch—"

"I *committed* to these dates months ago, because I'm an adult who makes plans and follows through with them."

"If I had known my mother was going to die—"

"It's not the money that kills me, it's what you're doing to Jimi. You told him that you guys would do something 'extra-special,' which I remember hoping meant more than going through the drive-through at Popeye's for a chicken sandwich."

Was it his fault that Jimi loved Popeye's more than the elevated version that Everett had created for him? The boy had inherited Clara's palate. "I get it."

"I'm not sure you do."

"I always *get it*, Clara."

"So then … you just *don't care*? You just always expect me to pick up the slack because your café is more important than my music career?"

"That's not what's happening here. My mom died, Clara. There's going to be a funeral."

"I think you said that."

"I wouldn't keep mentioning it if I felt like I was being heard."

"Don't get snippy with me, Everett."

"I barely raised my voice. You're the one who—"

"Great. The Blame Game. You're always looking for someone else to hold accountable, and you always have an excuse about how it's the universe's fault that you can't live up to your responsibilities. Instead of just doing the hard work of doing the hard work, you're always looking for a new person to fix your problems for you."

"That's not fair. You know I've been working on all of those things, Clara. You can't just expect me to change overnight."

"I don't expect you to change overnight."

"My mother died."

"I'm really sorry about that. But your son is alive, and he needs you to stop making excuses for why you can't be his father right now."

This was why their marriage had disintegrated. Because Clara couldn't stand it when his emotional needs took precedent over hers. She expected him to man up and move forward, no matter what happened. He was contractually obligated to be the strong one, because he was the husband, and she resented it when she had to be the supportive one for a couple of minutes.

The ice around his frozen heart grew thicker.

"You have every right to be angry," he forced himself to say. "Can I please come in and say goodnight to him?"

"He's in bed."

"Does that mean *no*?"

"You asked what time would be good for you to 'drop in.' I said 'seven.' I get a 'see you sevenish' back, then you show up here shortly after eight. *Which happens to be our son's bedtime.*"

"I know what happened," Everett said.

"You think I didn't hear you driving around the block,

blasting Radiohead, stalling until you knew Jimi would be asleep?"

"I was finishing a phone call," Everett lied, not quite brave enough to pretend that his imaginary call had to do with his mom's funeral, but hoping she'd assume it anyway. "Well, tell him I stopped by and that I'll see him soon."

"So, tell him, 'Daddy came by after your bedtime to tell us that he couldn't honor his commitment for this weekend?' Something like that?"

"Good night, Clara." Everett turned with a dramatic sigh.

"Good night, Everett."

He heard the door close behind him.

He got in his Aspire and pulled out his phone, not even caring if Clara was still watching.

Still nothing from his brothers.

What a couple of assholes. Their mother had died, and they were still ghosting him.

He deliberated on which of the Ds to call first, determined that it was Derek's turn, then said "Call Derek" as he started the car.

"Yo. Ev. Whatup?"

"Just leaving Clara's." Everett pulled into the street.

"You tell that little man I said *hi*?"

"He was already in bed. Clara was trying to punish me."

No response from Derek.

"So, are you sure you guys won't come to the funeral?" Everett asked.

"How many times are we gonna talk about this?"

"At least once more."

"We weren't invited to the funeral," Derek said. "And therefore, it isn't appropriate for us to go."

"It's bullshit that you guys weren't invited."

"I can't disagree. But put it out of your head, alright, man? Take care of yourself, and come see us when it's over. We'll be there for you … you know that, right?"

"Yeah," Everett said, feeling the edges of a smile. "I know."

"See you when I see you. I gotta hit the rituals."

"I hear you." Sort of.

But after Everett hung up, the temporary warmth of his friend's support faded in the chill of more ice. All Everett had ever wanted was his family's acknowledgement. His adopted father had only barely pretended to care while he was still alive. And so far, Cash had been unsuccessful in finding his biological family. If — *when* — his brothers excommunicated him, he would no longer have any family at all.

He drove the rest of the way home in silence, pondering the nature of loneliness. He didn't hear the texts when they came in, thanks to his leaving his phone on *Do Not Disturb* while driving. But his heart went buoyant when he picked it up to check after finding a parking spot two blocks from his shitty apartment building and saw a message from Roberto.

He felt a flicker of hope. But then he saw it was a link to an article: *7 Ways to Get Out of a Family Funeral (Without Feeling Guilty).*

Everett climbed the steps to his building, stomach in knots, thinking about how awful tomorrow would be.

Chapter Two

IT WAS A RUNNING joke that Everett would be late to his own funeral.

But it was even worse to be late while laying his mother to rest.

He couldn't even claim that an emergency had slowed him down. He'd barely slept last night, and woke up exhausted. Once dressed, he thought about cooking himself a hearty omelette, but the idea of spending more than a fleeting moment in the kitchen made him miss Mom too much.

So Everett got into his shit-heap Aspire and drove to get himself a dozen donuts instead. A dozen, because it made no sense to buy fewer once you ran the numbers. He hadn't meant to eat them all, but each one reminded him of her. The first time she'd made crullers for the school bake sale. The cake donuts they would make every summer and send with "the boys" when Dad got them up early to go fishing. The chocolate- and maple-glazed bars he'd helped her to frost for his brothers' soccer tournaments.

The final donut, a blueberry fritter, did him in. Or

maybe it was the knowledge that he was never going to turn around in the kitchen and see his mother sifting flour or dusting some new confection with powdered sugar. He'd stopped at a gas station to vomit the lot of them, then spent another quarter hour dabbing the splatters from his suit with a wet paper towel.

Now he was squeezing in for a seat as close to the front as he could get. No place for him in the family row. And Everett didn't think that was because he was late and his brothers hadn't saved him a seat. They would probably have kicked him out when they got there, even he'd been the first to arrive.

The church was gorgeous, filled with flowers in shades of white and cream, but Mom would have loved more color. She dressed in a rainbow, and insisted on the same when it came to ingredients in her kitchen. The bright green of a jalapeño, or the creamier shades of avocado. Red and orange peppers. Corn yellow and bone-white flour.

She would have appreciated how lush everything looked at her funeral. Because her family tree was full of peasants, Mom liked it when the world could see how far she had come. She would have loved the elaborate wreaths made from hundreds of roses.

You shouldn't have done all of this for me, he could imagine her saying, while enjoying every petal.

Everett took his seat, casually looking over at the family row again. Roberto turned around this time, then tapped Marco on the shoulder. They both looked over at him, Marco tapping at his watch while Roberto shook his head.

To hell with them; there wasn't a chance Everett would let them bully him away from her funeral. He didn't care what they said, or what *anyone* said: she was his mother, too.

Mom had been responsible for everything good in his life.

He wouldn't have a restaurant if it wasn't for her. Though Java Joe's was closer to the start of his dream than it was to the end of it. A simple coffee shop was the most overhead Everett could afford when starting out, but Joe's would be a real restaurant someday. The place just needed enough foot traffic to support the future expansion he had planned, along with a few other essential elements. Like a finalized menu and a kitchen staff. Plus, a kitchen.

It was a shame that Mom would never see the place finished. She was one of the only people who had ever really believed in his dream. Clara did, back in the beginning, before she got "burned out on it." The Ds always said they had faith in him, but Everett suspected that was only because they were his friends. His father had called Java Joe's "an idiot's fantasy" when it was still just a dream, and that was much nicer than most of the things his brothers had both whispered behind Everett's back and yelled out loud while laughing at him.

But Mom had never stopped believing. She'd made him into the chef he was today. The happiest times of his childhood were spent following her around the kitchen, learning her recipes, anticipating new flavors and discussing them in a way that neither of his other brothers ever could.

He wasn't so great at the business side of things, but fortunately he already knew which areas in the restaurant (still a coffee shop) required his attention. Now he just had to do the work. If there was a silver lining to this nightmare, at least now he would have a chance to fix what was broken.

When his father died a few years ago, Everett felt mostly a sense of relief, alongside a ravine of guilt for feeling any comfort in his passing. Legally, Jorge had three sons. But unlike Mom, he only had space in his heart for two — his "real" sons.

Roberto and Marco both took Dad's passing hard. And they'd taken their anger out on Everett, bullying him more ruthlessly than they had in high school.

They cornered him outside while Mom was soaking the casket with tears and told him to get lost, that he wasn't welcome at the wake.

The most humiliating part about it all was that he didn't even really blame them. He understood they'd been to Dad before Mom had brought Everett into the family. How could their adopted brother be anything but an intruder into their grief?

He felt the same way about Mom — like she'd been *his*, and he hated that he had to deal with them when he still couldn't even believe that he'd never see her again.

Another dirty look from his brothers, followed by horribly inappropriate snickering, then the priest approached the front pews with his raised hands and suggested that they get started.

Everett suffered through the introductory rite, the greeting and procession, then the congregation up the aisle. He ached during the sprinkling of holy water, the opening song and prayers, then all that reading from the Bible; Holy Communion followed by another assembly of prayers; the coffin taken back down the aisle and out of the church; graveside prayers for the rite of committal. Everything was punctuated by ugly glances from his brothers.

There wasn't a eulogy. Just the priest conducting his one-man show. Friends or family wanting to say a few words about the loss of their loved one would have to do so at the wake ... assuming they were invited.

Everett didn't consider himself Catholic. The religion

was just something else he accepted as the price of joining the family. Like the secret beatings. The stolen lunches. The humiliating rumors that everyone at school believed. Neither Marco nor Roberto were especially religious, but they were both always great at pretending. Probably because Catholicism had been a part of their lives since birth.

"Ximena Alvarez was so loving that she adopted an orphan in addition to raising her own." The priest looked out at Everett as if expecting him to genuflect.

A gallery of heads pivoted toward him, everyone wanting to see the adopted son displaying the appropriate level of gratitude.

He suffered through stares from the mourners and more recitations from the priest, until it was time for the procession of final farewells, where his brothers accepted condolences.

Everett waited his turn to say goodbye, feeling truly alone. He'd lived on the outskirts of this family, even during the best of times. Always the adopted child, as though nothing else about him mattered.

He stepped up to take his turn, resting a hand on the coffin and telling himself that he could do this as he looked down at his mom's frozen body. She would tell him to knock it off and remind himself what he had to be grateful for.

Everett wanted to say something, but Roberto and Marco were standing a few feet away, still in earshot, as if awaiting new ammunition — bullets of mockery and derision, right from the box. So he thought it to himself, hoping she'd hear up in heaven. *Thank you for sharing the best parts of yourself with me, Mom. I'll never stop cooking.*

It took all his courage, but Everett finally steeled himself and walked over to his brothers, surrounded by the same assembly of cousins, close friends, and family confidantes that always made him feel like the dimmest star, dying slowly just outside the constellation.

"Hey guys …" He nodded at his brothers, hoping that this setting and the small audience might be enough to curb their worst behavior.

"Have you tried the coffee?" Marco asked.

"No," Everett said, waiting for the punchline.

"Why don't you go grab one," Roberto suggested, looking around at the small circle of mourners. "Anyone else want a coffee?"

A few awkward demurrals and a lot of glances at the floor. This circle might not have been willing to stand up for the adopted Alvarez, or even liked Everett all that much, but at least they weren't participating in the cruelty.

"I'm not—"

But Roberto had already turned back to the group. "So, we were talking about Ensenada?"

"What's happening in Ensenada?" Everett dared to ask, already regretting his question. They clearly meant for him to find out whatever it was too late, forcing him to decide between the humiliation of staying home or the further embarrassment of showing up unwanted.

"Some of us are going down there in July …" said Madelina, Everett's adoptive second cousin.

"She means the family is going down there in July," Marco clarified.

"Our family," Roberto added.

The silence was long and heavy. Everyone was obviously waiting for Everett to leave. But instead of going, he gathered his courage and did the unthinkable.

"Do you mind if I have a minute to talk with my brothers alone?"

"Of course," Madelina said.

The crowd dispersed, leaving Everett alone with Marco and Roberto.

"You know what would make talking to this overweight pile of pubes feel less like ear rape?" Roberto asked his brother. The real one.

"A cup of coffee," Marco answered.

"Totally. Too bad the shit-whistle doesn't know how to listen."

"You didn't ask me to get you a cup of coffee, you suggested that I go and get one." His confidence was already gone. Why had he thought he could talk to them?

Roberto snorted. "The fuck do you want, Evie?"

"Please don't swear at me during Mom's funeral."

"*Please don't swear at me during Mom's funeral,*" Roberto repeated in a much higher pitch.

"Funeral's over, fuckface," Marco added.

Everett wanted to tell his brothers that he couldn't believe they were acting this way, and right now of all times, but the bitter truth was that their bad behavior wasn't surprising at all.

"Mom would want us to act like a family. We still have to interact with each other, you—"

"We do?" Marco feigned shock.

"Why?" Roberto asked.

"Even if you don't like it, we're still family."

"Close, but I would change that sentence to something like, *My family doesn't like me.*"

"Are we done here?" Marco asked.

"Please ... can we finally just ... get along for five minutes?" Everett felt himself breaking.

"Dude, be careful," Roberto told Marco. "I think this bag of dicks is about to cry."

"I wanted to talk to you about Mom's cookware—"

Marco replied in a stage whisper. "He doesn't really think he's getting anything, does he?"

Roberto nodded with considerable disbelief. "He might be that stupid."

Marco again: "Maybe we should clear that up."

So to Everett, Roberto said, "You're not getting *anything.*"

"You can't do that!" Everett hated himself for being so close to crying.

"We didn't do anything," Marco told him. "Well, except for the part where we handled Mom's estate."

"This isn't what she wanted!" Everett exclaimed. "Mom promised that she would leave me enough to turn Joe's around."

"Mom was too soft," Roberto said. "Papi wouldn't have wanted their money to go to waste."

"I have a lawyer, you know." Everett didn't, but what else could he say?

"Oh yeah?" Marco raised his eyebrows.

"Yeah," he lied again.

Roberto took the ball, glaring at Everett, the mirth now dead in his expression. "We're done here. Do you understand us?"

Everett couldn't talk without crying, so instead he shook his head.

"If we catch you near the house, either here or in Ensenada, or if you try any bullshit to contest the will, or anything else—"

"We'll show up at your shithole apartment in the middle of the night to remind you of who you are and where you really came from," Roberto finished.

"But she was my mother too!"

"Your mother is dead," Marco said.

"You were never really a part of this family." Roberto

looked like he wanted to spit. "And the one person in the world who made us pretend you were is no longer with us."

Everett would rather be naked than crying, but the tears came anyway. By voicing his biggest fear out loud, Roberto had turned it from a haunting into the truth.

The two assholes that he used to know turned their backs on him and started walking away.

Everett needed to get the fuck out of there fast.

He walked as fast as he could, outside of the church and over to his Aspire.

He climbed in, slammed the door, and finally allowed himself to sob like he wanted.

He checked his texts. A message from Cash might improve his mood. But there was nothing from him, or anyone else.

So Everett made a call before starting the engine.

It was Devon's turn to get him shitfaced.

Chapter Three

EVERETT WATCHED Derek's HardCorps character explode into a dust cloud of pixels onscreen.

Great. Now he would probably try to start talking again. The twins had been impressively patient so far, but would be ganging up on him soon.

But instead of saying anything, Derek stared at his tablet, watching Devon and Everett battling it out.

He and the twins loved playing games together. Everett had been planning on getting an Infinite Fidelity. After the Java Joe's project was paid for, of course. But now the newest gaming machine was just another dream.

He grabbed a handful of potato chips, shoved them into his mouth, then drowned his chewing in a fragrant wave of rum and Cherry Coke.

"Gross," Derek said, just like the last time.

Everett was grateful that the twins had both come over to play, but they weren't really there in the way he needed them to be. The Ds had both stopped drinking at one beer, while Everett kept refilling his own glass. He was far from drunk, still desperately seeking a buzz that seemed obnoxiously elusive. He wanted to smother everything he was feeling: grief that his mother was done, anger that his brothers managed to keep him from being closer to her even after her death, and the fear that this was not as bad as his life could get.

Since it was the day of his mother's funeral, the Ds weren't likely to accuse him of wallowing in self-pity. But he could feel that they were getting ready to go.

Devon died onscreen. Shit.

Everett slapped his thumb on *New Game* before either of the Ds could object.

Not that they would. Not today.

Everett grabbed his glass and drained it with a long swallow.

"Anyone else?" he asked them.

Derek looked at his brother on the sly, as if Everett couldn't see it. "No thanks, man. We gotta go soon."

"Of course." Everett hoped he didn't sound sarcastic. "You should both get home to your families. I seriously appreciate you coming over."

For a moment, it seemed like they were tempted. But their attention was back on the tablets.

Their characters donned parachutes onscreen, then walked to the edge of their shared chopper and jumped down from the heavens into the fray.

Everett hurried to catch up.

"So, how are things at Java Joe's?" Derek asked.

"You know." Everett shrugged, eyes on the screen, cycling through his inventory of weapons.

"What does that mean?" Devon asked.

Everett didn't answer either question, still staring at the screen as the countdown fell from three to one. So the twins tried a new topic.

Devon: "That sucks how your brothers are being their usual asshole selves."

Derek: "But that's not a surprise. We knew it was a probability."

Devon: "We talked about it just a couple of days ago."

Derek: "Then again yesterday."

Everett hated this. At least he was mowing through his enemies, with six kills already.

Devon: "Slow down."

Derek: "You're going to run out of ammo."

Devon: "Forget your brothers. You still need to come up with a plan for the Java Joe's situation."

"There is no *situation*," Everett said. "The restaurant is fine."

"Is it?" Devon asked.

"Come on, you guys." Everett shook his head and clenched his controller. "You always do this."

Devon looked at his brother, then at Everett. "What is it we do?"

"Waiting until I'm winning before you start talking?" But it came out too angry to sound like the joke he'd intended.

"We didn't wait to start talking, Everett. You waited to start being receptive."

"Until it was getting too late for a real conversation, because you knew we both had to go."

"That's not fair," Everett said.

"You're right," Derek agreed.

Devon: "Do you think maybe it's time to hang it up? Your apron, I mean."

Derek: "He's talking about the restaurant."

"Thanks." Everett rolled his eyes. "I've got it."

"You gave it your best shot," Devon continued, "but if

you don't have any money to rehab the business, then maybe—"

"Java Joe's doesn't have a substance abuse problem. It doesn't need rehab," Everett argued.

"You know what he means," Derek tried.

Everett didn't want to argue, so he opened another beer. "If I lose the restaurant, then I won't have anything left of Mom's legacy."

Especially since Marco and Roberto were determined to keep him from inheriting the pots and pans she'd cooked with. Those assholes would probably donate them to charity, just to spite him.

The twins traded a look. Everett wasn't sure if he wanted to kick his friends out or beg them to stay. Might as well take another drink.

Devon shrugged. "We support your trying to recoup the restaurant ... if you have a plan. But no offense, we've never actually heard you tell us what your strategy might be."

"Well, it doesn't really matter now, does it?" Everett asked, not really wanting an answer. "No need for you guys to worry about me, I'll figure something out."

Derek: "If there's no need for us to worry about you, then why aren't we home right now?"

Devon: "He means that we're here for you, we just—"

"I know what he means." Everett hated when the Ds did this. It was all fun and games until they started using their *wonder twin powers, activate* energy against him. "The restaurant isn't just about me, you know. It's about not giving up."

Derek: "It's not giving up if you're moving on with intention."

Devon: "Just think about all the other things you could do with the same time. You keep thinking that Joe's is gonna give you this great life, when maybe it's the thing that's been holding you back."

"Java Joe's isn't holding me back." Everett wanted to put on a brave face, or make a joke to prove he was fine. Instead he said, "Do we have to talk about this on the day of my mother's funeral?"

The Ds were dead again, but he was still on a roll and fighting to stay alive, knowing this was it for the night. Once Everett was dead on screen, his friends would be leaving in real life.

At least he would finally be out of this awkward conversation, where the twins were yet again trying to convince him to give up on his dream. How could they possibly understand? The Ds had their families.

Without his restaurant, Everett had nothing.

A sniper must have been hiding in the bell tower, because as soon as he rounded the corner, Everett's character took a bullet to the head, then evaporated in high definition.

"Time to go?" Everett asked, the hope for one last round like sugar in his voice.

"You always do this," Derek said.

"What do I do?"

"You wait forever to have a real conversation," Devon replied.

"That's not true." Everett started a new game … just in case they wanted to.

"You know it is," Derek argued.

"We're always here for you, and we want to help, but it's not like you ever take our advice."

"I take your advice all the time." Everett still sounded like he was pouting, even though he was only stating an obvious fact. "You're both always acting like I can't take care of myself."

Another one of those quiet looks passed between the twins, and they powered off their tablets in tandem, then packed them into their respective bags, like the mirror images of each other that they were.

"One more?" He hoped his request didn't sound like begging. Because that's not what this was at all; Everett was only making the Ds an offer.

"Alright, one more." Devon surprised him by pulling his tablet back out of his bag and turning it on just as Everett's character was about to jump from the chopper.

Derek joined him. "But only if you listen instead of talking while we kick your ass."

"He doesn't know how to listen."

"I know how to listen just fine." Everett shrugged. "Go ahead and say whatever you want."

All three of them leaped out of the helicopter.

Devon began the assault. "You're not taking care of yourself, man."

"Look at this place." Derek moved his head around to indicate Everett's apartment, but his eyes stayed fixed to the tablet. "It's disgusting."

Devon: "Seriously, what's wrong with you? Don't you have a laundry basket?"

Derek: "You are what you eat, man."

Devon: "And you're eating too much junk."

Derek: "That's why you're gaining so much weight."

"Maybe I've gained a few pounds," Everett said. "But I've been stressed out."

Devon: "I thought you weren't going to talk?"

Derek: "We're both married with children. Doesn't stop us from staying cut."

Devon: "Just takes a little work."

"Easy for you to say. You guys have great genetics."

Everett squinted at the screen. He'd taken a lot of damage, thanks to the twins distracting him.

Derek: "We work hard."

Devon: "Hitting the gym at least three times a week has nothing to do with genetics."

"My parents were both probably predisposed to obesity," Everett said, dragging out one of his dustiest arguments. "It's actually impressive that I'm as lean as I am."

"*Lean?*" Derek repeated.

Devon just laughed.

As much as he hated being ridiculed, but it was still better than being alone. One more hit and his character was dead. Maybe two. Then his best — really his *only* friends — would be gone.

It was strange to feel jealous of people who he loved so much. Everett preferred not to see his emotion as envy, but more as an acknowledgement that Derek and Devon shared something he longed for, something they'd had since the day he met them: that psychic link that twins shared in movies, TV, and comic books. They went halfsies on all of their clothes and took tests for each other. Their skill sets and interests were neatly divided, so Devon could always take care of their English homework, while Derek handled the math.

The Ds had been there for Everett through the incessant bullying and his frustration with dating. They hadn't judged him when he dropped out of college, and they were his best men when he married Clara. They'd sympathized when that marriage ended in divorce, and empathized as he'd struggled to keep Java Joe's alive after a Hill of Beans opened up a block away.

Everett's character died again.

"FUCK!" He dropped his controller onto the coffee table.

The brothers laughed, and yeah, they could go.

Everett stood from the couch to walk his friends to the door. Only after standing upright did he realize how thoroughly fuckered he was.

"Wow," he said, trying to regain his balance. *"I'm drunk."*

"Mission accomplished." Derek slipped the tablet into his bag.

"Call us tomorrow," Devon said.

"Yeah. Sure." Everett felt like he was about to throw up.

Derek opened the door and turned back around, as if something had just occurred to him. "Hey, whatever happened with that P.I. you were talking to?"

"Yeah, anything happen with that?"

"Nothing so far." Then, since the Ds were still on the right side of his door, Everett made them an offer. "Why don't you stay ... just another hour? I could make—"

Devon shook his head and put a kind hand on Everett's shoulder. "We'll check in with you tomorrow. Cool?"

No, it wasn't cool at all. But Everett's head was spinning and his mother was dead and the only thing he had to remember her by was the café driving him into bankruptcy. And there was nothing the Ds could do about any of it. So he thanked them for hanging out and shut the door.

Now he was alone in his slobby apartment, to contemplate the emptiness of a future without the only person who'd ever loved him.

Or if he got a little drunker, he could pass out on the couch and not have to think about any of this for a few hours.

As he grabbed a beer and sat down, his phone buzzed on the coffee table.

He looked at the screen, surprised to see the text he'd been waiting for.

A message from Cash: *I got the info you've been wanting. Meet in person tomorrow?*

Yeah, if he was still alive.

Chapter Four

"I REALLY THINK we should call a plumber," Lena said again, clearly expecting Everett to have somehow come up with more money since the last time.

He shook his head. "I already told you that we can't afford it right now."

Everett didn't want to have this conversation. Cash would be here any minute.

"And I already told you: *I'm not a plumber.*" She followed his gaze to the door. "Are you expecting someone?"

"I don't know why you're acting like this is such a big deal. It's not like I'm asking you to install a bathtub, Lena. It's a little leak, no big deal."

"Yeah, no big deal. I'm sure a plumber could fix it in a few minutes."

Even if he had the money to pay a plumber, it was still Lena's job to do whatever the boss told her to do.

Gavin Cash entered Joe's and claimed a seat over at the end of the small bar.

"We can deal with this later, okay? I need to go and talk to that guy."

"So, what am I supposed to do about the leak?"

"Just ignore it for now."

"But it's getting worse," she replied.

"It's not like we have any customers right now. See if you can google an answer or something."

"Or I could call a plumber," Lena suggested again.

He ignored her comment, approaching Cash, who stood to greet him with his hand extended to a shake. Everett led the P.I. to a small table, away from the coffee bar, just out of earshot from Lena and everyone else.

Cash dropped a green file folder on the table as they both sat.

Everett was dying to know what might be waiting inside. After two weeks of waiting, had Cash finally found Everett's real parents? Ironic that he might finally find them mere days after losing the last of his adoptive mom and dad.

This might be the thing that turned his life around.

"Thanks for coming," Everett said.

"Thanks for paying me." Cash's dirty-blond hair hung in a curtain to his chin. His easy smile appeared to hold an infinity of secrets. He always had a week's worth of stubble, despite the time or day, and perhaps the coolest disposition Everett had ever seen. "You the sort fellow who likes to start with the good or the bad?"

"You have both?"

Gavin gave him a knowing smile. "I usually do."

Everett had fantasized about a happy reunion with his long-lost parents for most of his life.

Mom had always discouraged his quest. She said that he was an Alvarez now, so his origin didn't matter. But she was the only one in the family who had ever really given a shit about him. His brothers had made sure he would never feel like an Alvarez.

Now he was seconds from an answer that might mend the broken parts of his life. At the same time, he couldn't help but worry. What if his biological parents still didn't want anything to do with him?

"Let's start with the bad news." Everett gave him a nod.

There was a gushing sound from behind the counter, then Lena was at their table. "Sorry to interrupt. It's getting worse."

"I'll deal with it later, after my meeting is over."

"Whatever," Lena said, with enough sass for an immediate firing.

He'd deal with her later too.

"So ... bad news first ..." Everett reminded Cash once Lena had retreated behind the counter. Then, before the P.I. had a chance to respond: "Can I get you a coffee or anything?"

"I'm good, thanks." A light smile, then the P.I. cleared his throat. "Unfortunately, both of your biological parents are deceased."

Great, Everett thought — *0 for 4.*

"Your parents were young when they had you. Your mother was a year older than your father at sixteen. They both came from broken homes. and neither of them had the support or resources to take care of you. The details are all in there."

Cash slid the green folder across the table to Everett. "In short, your dad died in a drunk driving accident a month before you were born. Your mom gave you up for a closed adoption, and passed from diabetes-related complications. On your third birthday as it turns out."

"*Diabetes-related complications?* But she was so young ..." Everett had been right: the Ds really did have all the genetic luck.

"I'm sorry. I know that's not what you wanted to hear."

No, it wasn't. But there was zero chance Everett was going to let the P.I. see how heartbroken he was. The fairy-tale reunion with a loving family that regretted giving him up was something he'd never experience.

It was hard enough to understand why a mother would ever want to give up her child, but he'd always had an even harder time understanding why someone would adopt a child they had no intention of loving. Could Jorge Alvarez have loved another orphan, and Everett was really that unlovable?

If his adopted father had cared about him enough to set the proper example, then surely Marco and Roberto would have too.

"And the good news?"

Cash pointed to the folder. "You rather hear it or read it?"

Everett felt hopeful. The P.I.'s face promised not just good news, but *great* news. "Why don't you tell me?"

"You have a brother."

"A brother?" Everett repeated with inspired disbelief. "You mean a half-brother?"

"I mean a twin."

"A twin!" Everett was suddenly out of his seat.

He couldn't believe this. Gavin might as well have said that he was actually born on a tiny little planet called Krypton.

Everett sat back down. "Are you fucking with me?"

Again Cash gestured at the folder. "The details are in there. But rest assured, I am most certainly not fucking with you. Evan Shepherd, your identical twin, lives in Austin, Texas."

"You've gotta be kidding me." Everett couldn't believe his luck. This might be the best day of his entire life. "I've always felt like maybe I had a twin." He picked up the folder, but didn't yet open it. "Why weren't we adopted together?"

"The adoption agency knew they'd have a hard time placing twins, so they split you up to give you both a better chance."

"This is unbelievable." He shook his head, smile still wide enough to make his face ache. He barked laughter as he leafed through the folder. Two pages — the first with a few bullet points about his biological parents, and the second with some particulars about his biological brother. He looked back up at Cash. "Is this all you have?"

"I'm happy to dig some more, but I know cost is a factor. So I figured—"

"I can take it from here."

"Understood." The P.I. nodded, then leaned across the table. "Mind if I give you some free advice?"

"Please," Everett said.

"I can see that you're happy to hear you have family and—"

"I can't believe his name is Evan. It's so close to Everett."

"I've seen a lot of this in my line of work," he tried again.

"A lot of family reunions, you mean?"

"A lot of people who didn't want to be found."

Everett looked back at Gavin, baffled. "Why wouldn't my brother want to be found?"

"I'm not saying he doesn't want to be, I'm just saying you can't make any assumptions and—"

"But we're *twins.* Don't you know what that means?"

"I think I can guess what you want it to mean." The P.I. smiled as he stood. "Give me a call if you need anything. I'm happy to help if I can."

For a price, he didn't have to add.

"Thanks so much." Everett waved the folder like a victory flag. "For all of this."

Cash agreed to a cup of coffee to go, then left Everett with a two-fingered salute.

"Great, your boyfriend is gone." Lena rushed over before the door had closed behind him. "We have a problem."

"What now?"

"The kitchen is flooding."

"Did you google it?" Everett asked.

"You've gotta be fucking kidding me."

"You shouldn't swear at your boss."

"ARE YOU GOING TO DO ANYTHING TO HELP ME?"

She was right, he *should be* helping her with this mess. But right now there was nothing more important than learning more about his twin brother.

"Fine. You can hire a plumber."

"*You* can hire a plumber."

"Something's come up and I have to go."

"No way. You can't—"

"It's urgent. Family business."

"I quit."

"What?" Everett exclaimed. "You can't quit."

"You must mean that I can't quit more than once. But just for shits and grins: *I quit.* There, I did it again, even if it didn't matter the second time."

"You can't quit. I need you."

"Then maybe you should pay me more than minimum wage."

"Plus tips!"

"Which amount to almost nothing, because you won't

take any of my suggestions for bringing in more customers." Lena took off her apron.

"You can have a dollar more per hour, starting next paycheck."

"Two dollars, starting this paycheck."

"I really can't do that." Everett shook his head. "You know how much this place is making."

"Your lack of business acumen isn't my problem. Not anymore. Raise revenue by $40 a day and you can pay me another $16. If you can't do that, then—"

"Fine: $1.50 more an hour starting next paycheck, then $2.00 as soon as possible after that." Then, before she could answer. "Payroll is already called in for this period, so it has to be your next paycheck, no matter what."

"Thirty days. Then it's $2.00 more or I'm out of here. And you need to start listening to me when—"

"You're right, I don't listen enough. Your ideas are great." He glanced back at the door. "But I really have to go. You've got this? With the plumber?"

She sighed. "Do I have a choice?"

"Thank you. I'll be in later today, or probably tomorrow."

"Whenever, dude."

"You just got a raise," Everett said, turning to go. "You should be smiling."

Lena was right, about how much better the business needed to be.

But soon all the stuff that had been holding him back no longer would be.

Once he connected with his honest-to-God twin brother, nothing would hold him back ever again. Because for the first time in his life, Everett wouldn't be alone.

Happy birthday to me.

Chapter Five

THIS WAS the best and worst birthday week of his life.

Everett had been floating when he left the café, but as he tried to rehearse the start of a phone call with his brother, the sickness in the pit of his stomach intensified. There was no way he could focus on cooking, especially with Mom's death still bobbing on the surface.

So he stopped on his way home to pick up a pizza and an order of cinnamon dippers — a little comfort food to settle his nerves. It didn't beat Mom's machaca tacos, but what did? Maybe the gourmet mac-and-cheese that the Ds kept trying to get him to stop making. But even that dish reminded him of Mom, because it was his first original recipe, and she'd called him her little chef after tasting it.

The discovery of a twin brother should have made him feel less alone instead of even lonelier. And it would, eventually. But right now, as he sifted through Evan's various social media feeds, he was consumed with jealousy. Especially when it came to his brother's *restaurants* — apparently one success wasn't enough, because his twin was about to open a second one. Not a second location, either, but a completely different restaurant, with its own menu and theme.

Evan also had a gorgeous wife, two kids, and a stunning custom house, a far cry from the McMansions that Everett saw as one of the few benefits of living in a flyover state. With all Evan had going for him, it was hard to understand why he chose to live in Texas, of all places. That was the one area where life had given Everett the upper hand.

In every other way, Evan's resume read like proof that the universe had used the same deck to deal two extremely different hands. They both had restaurants, but while Java Joe's was barely holding on (and arguably, not even a restaurant), Evan's first restaurant, Señor Sushi, was a massive success.

Everett had managed to cobble together just over twenty grand with a combination of loans from Mom and the Ds, while Evan's first restaurant had been opened with a million in seed money.

With such a strong start, it was no surprise that Señor Sushi won an award its first year. Nor was it surprising that when beloved Austin-based actor Miles McCafferty said it was his favorite new place to eat in the city, Señor Sushi had a line out the door. That wouldn't have been possible in Las Orillas, since celebrity sightings so close to Los Angeles was more like spotting stars in the sky.

Everett wanted to know all there was about his biological soulmate, but he'd hit a wall on what was publicly available. Cash could have thrown in a simple background check, considering what Everett had spent. But it only ran thirty bucks, so he paid the fee to run the check himself.

He wasn't sure if he should feel relieved or disappointed. Evan Shepherd of Austin, Texas had never suffered so much as a parking ticket.

He clicked back over to LiveLyfe, navigating through his brother's profile again while pondering the nature of twins. He'd seen how remarkable the twin connection could be with the Ds, so he knew the psychic bond was a genuine thing. But now looking through the many parallels of their separate lives, the proof was irrefutable. In a few ways the two men's' existences seemed to be spitting images of each other. Or rather, Everett's life appeared like a bootleg of his brother's much better thing.

Evan had married a Klair to Everett's Clara, although Evan was still married where Everett was not. Klair and Clara were both musicians, still playing in bands. And both brothers loved cooking enough to become chefs — what were the odds?

He went down a rabbit hole, researching facts about twins in general. Everything suddenly made sense, the elements of a life spent mostly lost, finally arranging themselves into order.

Twins shared an unbreakable bond because their relationship started in utero. Researchers had studied fetuses at just fourteen weeks old with video taken from 3D ultrasounds. Twins were shown reaching out for each other, and having "appreciable physical contact" more than twenty percent of the time. Twins interacted socially with one another hours after birth, *because they were wired to do so.*

No wonder Everett had lived an entire lifetime feeling like something was missing.

Because something *always* had been.

No doubt Evan had felt the same thing lacking in his life, despite the success. How many nights had each of them lain awake, wondering what it would be like to fill that hole in their souls, without realizing the other was out there doing the same thing?

He clicked over to the Señor Sushi tab and started

browsing the restaurant, investigating both its menu and decor. Japanese dishes, made with a Tex-Mex flavor palette. A novel concept, and Everett could see why it worked. Slightly surprising for Texas, but Austin was supposedly more open-minded than most other Southern cities. The place looked fancy, but not ostentatious. Pricey without being prohibitive. Trendy, yet not obnoxious. And reading a few of the featured reviews revealed something interesting. It wasn't just the restaurant, or the food. People loved the proprietor. Austin appreciated Evan's restaurant, and was clearly eager to see what Everett's brother might do next.

Señor Sushi has the best recipes, the most crazy-amazing plating, and with Evan Shepherd, one of the city's greatest restaurateurs. ~ *Josiah Beck, Austin Eats Well.*

Evan Shepherd has put every Tex-Mex restaurant in Austin on notice: Señor Sushi is A+ eating. ~ *Gracy Kern, Eatz Alive.*

If Tequila Mockingbird is half the restaurant that Señor Sushi has turned out to be, we're in for another groundbreaking culinary experience. ~ *Sarah Carney, Dished*

One successful restaurant with another on the way. Plus a wife and two kids. But Everett had nothing to be envious about. Evan probably hadn't had a moment of free time in years. Video games were among the listed hobbies on his brother's LiveLyfe page, including Hard-Corps, but Evan's favorite character was cancelled three versions ago. It might be up to Everett to teach his brother how to relax and enjoy life again.

He followed a link from Señor Sushi to a landing page for Tequila Mockingbird. Evan's new restaurant would be opening in a couple of weeks, and while there wasn't a menu, the *coming soon* copy sounded delicious. A lot more up Everett's alley. Less of a novelty, with authentic recipes from the Gulf of Mexico reimagined for a modern palate.

The Gulf of Mexico is home to some of the world's greatest flavors, and soon Tequila Mockingbird will be home to the greatest flavors from the Gulf. The balmy, easygoing region boasts a rich cuisine with a blend of Caribbean, Afro-Cuban and Spanish flavors influenced by Havana, San Juan, Cartagena and New Orleans. Mingling with the better-known savory tastes of Mexican food, the indigenous palate includes corn, vanilla, acuyo and hoja santa herbs, supplemented by a wide variety of tropical and citrus fruits such as papaya, mamey, and zapote.

You won't believe what we're doing with seafood! Reserve your seats for the opening of Tequila Mockingbird now!

Good for Evan. It was amazing to think that people were making reservations for a restaurant that wasn't even open yet, especially considering Everett couldn't even figure out how to raise his revenue by another $40 a day. *Yet.*

He clicked away from the Tequila Mockingbird landing page and back over to LiveLyfe to learn more about Klair. In so many ways she seemed like a prettier, more successful version of Clara. Her band, All Sounds Considered, was gaining impressive traction. They'd been live-streaming shows on Tuesday nights for several months. Their last one had more than 20,000 *live* viewers, and had been viewed a quarter million times since. By contrast, Clara's band had slightly less than 20,000 views on their most popular performance.

More comments, more likes, more merch, and more fandom all around.

But that wasn't even the thing that would really get to Clara if she were to see what Everett was looking at now. Klair's life appeared effortlessly glamorous.

Clara would be jealous when she found out.

Everett felt bad looking through her profile, seeing

Klair and Evan celebrate their successes as a happy couple, arms around each other in every shot.

It was probably a lot easier to support your wife's endeavors when you had victories of your own. Everett felt equally inspired and jealous — even more so when he looked at his niece and nephew's profiles.

His niece and nephew were overachievers in every measurable way, and Klair was constantly crowing about it. Evan must be so proud of them.

He refused to compare them to his son, Jimi, who got average grades and spent a lot of his time reading really nerdy books.

He closed his laptop. Because the more he learned about his brother's life, the less it felt like looking in a mirror. Seeing Evan's picture next to his was like staring at a side-by-side comparison of Andy Dwyer and Star Lord.

It was easier to eat comfort food after cooking all day for unappreciative customers who couldn't tell the difference between a gourmet quiche and the much cheaper garbage they could get at the big chains. Sure, Everett's food cost more, because he used real ingredients, and he had to eat the cost of the unsold inventory.

It was easier to play video games with his son on the weekends instead of teaching him how to cook — he was exhausted by Friday and Jimi just wanted to escape from homework. Anyone in his position would do the same.

And it was easier to let Clara go than fight to keep her, because she'd never understood his dedication to making the restaurant work. She could never quite get that he was working for *them*, to make Joe's successful enough that they could live the life they'd always wanted.

Everett and his brother had started their existence with the same exact canvas, but Evan's life had afforded him what appeared to be ten times as many colors and brushes.

Greater in number, but also richer in depth, texture, and overall quality. No wonder he'd painted a much better picture.

Everett might have been the Andy Dwyer to Evan's Star Lord, but he told himself that he felt inspired instead of envious. He had seen irrefutable proof of his potential, and was determined to never shortchange himself again.

In Evan's perfect life, Everett had found a blueprint for his own success.

Chapter Six

EVERETT WATCHED THE Ds' wives herding their children from the play area to the picnic tables, while he struggled to hide his irritation with his two best friends.

"That is, without a doubt, the worst idea you've ever had," Devon said.

"No way," Derek disagreed. "That is the worst idea anyone has ever had."

"It's my brother's birthday."

Derek jabbed a finger at his chest. "No, it's *your* birthday. You're doing this for *you*."

"I'm doing it for both of us! Finding out you have a long-lost brother on your birthday is like the best present ever."

"Yeah," Devon agreed … sort of. "For you."

"So, let me get this straight," Derek said, turning to face Everett straight on. "You're planning on driving to Austin to surprise your twin brother on his birthday. A man, whom despite your genetic connection you have no relationship with whatsoever—"

"—And you're going to do this without calling him,

sending an email, or even a carrier pigeon to let him know you exist. That about right?" Devon finished what Derek had started.

"*Our* birthday," Everett said again. "Maybe you guys don't understand this because you've known each other for your entire lives. But try to imagine you'd been separated at birth. Wouldn't you want to know if you had a twin brother?"

"Not without a phone call first," replied the brothers in unison.

"I don't understand why you guys won't just drop it."

Derek looked at his brother. "What do you think, should we let this go?"

"Absolutely not." Devon turned to Everett. "What if he's not home?"

"He'll be home, okay? It's his birthday. He won't go out of town to celebrate, because he has a restaurant to run, and a new one to open. Trust me, we never get time off in this business."

The Ds traded a look. Everett ignored it.

"Seriously. I don't see why it's so hard for you guys to go with me on this. There's always been a hole in my life … for as long as I can remember. Now I *finally* understand why. I *felt* like I was missing a brother, but now I *know*. What if Evan feels the same way? What if I'm changing his life as much as I'm changing mine?"

Derek sighed. "Look man, we get it. For real—"

"You think your brother's gonna be doing backflips on Jupiter once he finds out he has a twin—"

"And we'd want to think the same thing too—"

"But you can't automatically assume that he has the same void in his life. You're different people."

"I'm not 'assuming' anything," Everett interrupted

Derek to get a word in. "I just wish you guys were happy for me."

Devon: "We're happy for you, but it's not like you're telling us that you found out you had a brother and now you're going to send the dude an email."

Derek: "You're driving halfway across the country in a twenty-year-old Ford Aspire. Which is, in itself, a terrible idea."

"Not everyone can afford to drive a brand new Outback." Everett looked from Devon to Derek. "Or a *Mustang.*"

"I told you, the Mustang is part of my job," Derek said.

"The Outback is a perfect car," Devon added.

"Like Donaldson is the perfect quarterback." Derek laughed again.

"You don't *need* a Mustang," Everett argued. "You just think it looks cool."

"I work with athletes. They respect my vehicle of choice."

"I'm with Everett on this one," Devon pressed. "You'd be better off in a—"

"Jessa!" Derek smiled at the sudden appearance of his wife, taking her hands as she approached them. "We were just finishing up."

"I hope so. If the kids get any hungrier, we'll have a riot on our hands."

Jessa turned from Derek to Everett. "Did he tell you that Mia and Maya were each student of the month, back-to-back?"

"He doesn't want to hear that," Derek told her.

"He's your friend. Of course he does. Don't you, Everett?"

"Of course I do." And he did.

But as happy as Everett always was for his friends, the

envy was there. Not only were the Ds lucky enough to have been born with one another in their lives from day one, they both now had wonderful wives and children of their own.

Everett finally had a chance to have what the Ds had.

Jessa nudged her husband on the shoulder. "I don't know why you're being so shy."

Derek smiled, looking awkward and uncertain, but then his body straightened and his expression brightened. "Mia got it last month, and we just heard that it's Maya now. The big deal is that their school does a terrific job with expecting kids to really earn things, you know?"

"No participation awards," Jessa explained.

"Right," Derek continued, now beaming. "There are nine spots for the whole year, and our girls got two of them. We're so proud."

"Isn't first grade a little young for student of the month?" Everett asked.

"Damn right, first grade is a little young for student of the month," Derek agreed.

"Honey, language." Jessa gave him a playfully admonishing look.

"Sorry." Derek kissed her on the cheek. "We'll be right there."

"You all ready to eat?" Devon asked.

Everett looked over at the table. Everything came in sets. The brothers, the wives, the twins, and the siblings. Everett wasn't just a third wheel, he was an unwanted unicycle lying on its side, unloved and abandoned in the corner.

"You know what," Everett said, surprising himself. "I'm sick of always feeling like a third wheel."

"You're one of the family," Devon replied. "If you're not feeling it, that's on you."

"It's always on me."

"That's an example of a man-child feeling sorry for himself right there." Derek laughed.

But it wasn't funny. "I'm serious. You guys have no idea what it's like to live as an outsider. You each have a built-in best friend, and no matter how much you might disagree about Mustangs or Outbacks, you're always connected. You claim you can't read each other's minds, but you obviously share some sort of instinctive emotional connection. You take the blame for each other, have icebreakers for every conversation—"

"You're right about all of that stuff ..." Devon said to Everett. "But it's not because we're twins, it's because we've grown up together. You're imagining that you can copy-and-paste the relationship Derek and I have into a relationship with a brother you just found out about a few hours ago. And I'm afraid you'll be disappointed when it doesn't go down like that."

Derek turned to Everett. "Look. I know you don't want to hear this, but as your friends, it's our job to be real with you." He paused to look at Devon, using his psychic twin energy to say, *I got this.* Then he continued.

"You've got a lot of stuff to sort out right now. Reach out to your new brother — *absolutely.* We can sit down and I'll help you figure out what to say if you'd like. Take this one step at a time."

Jessa looked over.

Derek gave her a nod. "We should go."

Devon said, "Look, man, all we're saying is that you should focus on getting your life together before reaching out to your brother."

"That's what you're not getting. Reaching out to Evan is what's going to turn my luck around."

Derek glanced at the picnic table again, then back at

Devon. "He's not going to hear you. Let's eat."

But Devon couldn't let it go. "You remember that time you bought that online course promising to solve all your problems? New U?"

Derek: "Of course he remembers. He paid a thousand dollars for it."

"You're right, Devon. I can totally see how my finding out I have a brother and wanting to connect with him is the same as buying an online course—"

"For a thousand dollars," Derek interjected.

"—because I wanted to invest in my self-improvement."

"But that's just it," Devon said. "You were never investing in your self-improvement, you were trying to buy an easy button. You have exactly the same problems now as you did before you bought the course."

They couldn't understand, because they already had the thing he needed. It was like water to a fish for them. But he couldn't say that without being accused of pouting.

The Ds looked at him.

He gave them his very best smile. "Sorry for being a downer. Let's eat."

"Hey, man, you're grieving, no need to apologize," Derek said. "We're just watching out for you."

The picnic spread was amazing, but Everett felt sick to his stomach. He fumbled through an awkward goodbye as soon as he could, then rolled away like the crooked third wheel that he was.

Everett began to feel better once he was home, eating the burger and onions rings he'd picked up on the way. He felt a twinge of guilt — would Evan eat at Sloppy's, or whip up a gourmet burger? Probably the latter, and once Everett's life was back in balance, so would he. There were a million things to do before hitting the road, so saving time made the most sense.

He could hardly wait to cook alongside his brother.

He should tell Clara, and say goodbye to Jimi. Except that Clara would say the same things that the Ds had, but with more swearing.

He would be back soon enough. And it would be so much easier to tell her where he'd been when he could also introduce Jimi to his Uncle Evan and Aunt Klair, and his cousins, Harmony and Jazz.

Packing made him feel better. Everett imagined the drive and all the time he would have to think about improving his life on the way to Austin, where he would knock on Evan's door and introduce himself to his long-lost twin.

Evan was the key that would unlock the higher levels of Everett's life.

Chapter Seven

FOUR HOURS DOWN, eighteen to go. Everett was bored as hell.

He planned to drive all night and show up in the early morning on his birthday, so that he and his brother would have the whole day to celebrate together.

Not his birthday, *their* birthday. He should really start thinking in pairs. That was his life now. Everett was one half of a matching set. Always had been and always would be.

He was starting to worry about the heat. The Aspire's AC didn't work especially well under the best of circumstances, and it definitely wasn't up to the challenge of holding back the Arizona burn. Everett was trying to see how long he could go without turning it on, saving his AC for a stretch of what he thought of as Dead Man's Walk to get through in New Mexico. It would be the death of him to end up stranded on the lonely highway without air conditioning.

He stared at the FedEx truck in front of him and shifted his thoughts into another gear. He imagined swimming in his brother's pool as they compared childhoods and planned for a future together. Would Evan want to move out to Los Orillas? Probably. No doubt he'd stayed in Austin by default, because that's where his adoptive parents had chosen to live. It wasn't always easy to leave the garden where you originally grew, even if the place was full of weeds that needed to get yanked out by the root. Everett knew that from experience.

And that got him thinking, did he have another family now? Were Evan's parents now his parents too?

On one hand, he loved the idea. More family.

But on the other, Everett had nothing to share in return. His brothers wanted nothing to do with him, so they sure as hell wouldn't want anything to do with Evan.

The Ds would welcome Evan into their lives.

Everett wiped the sweat from his eyes again and conceded defeat. He felt like he was on the edge of heatstroke.

Dammit. He turned on the AC, mopped the puddle of sweat from his brow, and got back to thinking.

Where was he?

They were both restaurateurs, so maybe they could open a place together in Las Orillas. It could even be twin-themed. But not cheesy. No Dollywood vibes or anything like that. Their place would be classy, reservations only and always a waiting list. Authentic Mexican food only. Maybe the twin hook could be in the plating. Every dish had a yin and a yang. From chips and salsa to corn and flour.

Unless Everett was getting it totally wrong.

The more he explored the idea, the more he doubted himself. He hadn't been this uncomfortable in a long time. He wanted to pull off the highway and get something to eat. Stretch his legs. Turn the podcast up so he could get the questions out of his head.

What if he's not home?

What are you saying to Clara and Jimi?

Maybe you should work on your issues at home before driving out to Austin?

The Ds might be right; Everett might be making a big mistake.

It wasn't too late to turn around.

Except that he would feel the humiliation forever.

And Everett wasn't a quitter. Not anymore.

But maybe it was weird to appear unannounced, even if he was showing up with the best possible news.

He didn't even have a gift.

What if gaining a brother wasn't enough of a present?

Obviously, it wasn't. Evan would probably feel blind-sided at first. His family definitely would, too.

A gift for all of them — something that would allow Everett to join in the fun as the newest member of the family.

Maybe a croquet set?

No, that would be dumb, the kids were teenagers. And Evan was so successful. What would he not already have that Everett could afford?

It was also intimidating how well Evan had done. He didn't brag about it on Livelyfe, but his wife did, in a #blessed way.

Her gorgeous kitchen, the pool, and an elegant guest house behind the main house. Their rooms were filled with things Everett didn't have and couldn't buy. Every one of the three cars in their driveway made his Aspire look like it belonged in a junkyard.

What could he possibly give to a family like that?

As if by magic, the billboard ahead announced a Tucson mall at the next exit. Perfect. He'd lose a little time, but that would be worth it if he was getting a gift for the person who was about to change his life.

Happy birthday to both of them.

But at the mall, Everett discovered that his time scrolling through Livelyfe hadn't really told him anything about his brother's likes and dislikes. A generic gift like wine wouldn't feel special enough to reflect the deep connection he wanted Evan to feel.

He should get back on the road and use all that alone time in the car to think up the a present.

But on the way to the exit, Everett realized he'd been thinking about the gift in the wrong way. If he wanted to find something that embodied their twin connection, he needed only to ask what *he* would want.

The answer came immediately — the new virtual reality gaming system, Infinite Fidelity. They could get to know each other while playing HardCorps together — Everett helping Evan remember how to have fun, while Evan shared the secrets of his success.

Even better, every time he ever played with the Infinite Fidelity, either now in the future, alone or with his family, Evan would think of his twin brother.

Five hundred bucks wasn't exactly cheap, but this was a momentous occasion. A once-in-a-lifetime happening.

Everett went the nearest directory, found Gameway on the map, and nearly cheered when he saw that the store was right behind him.

He locked eyes with the clerk as he entered. "I'd like an Infinite Fidelity, please."

"Sure," she said, with zero emotion, accent, or affect. "With or without the game bundle?"

"How much is it with the game bundle?"

"$799."

"Without, please."

"With or without the warranty?"

"How much is the warranty?"

"$149."

"Without, please. How many headsets and controllers does it come with?"

She looked at Everett as if he were either nuts or an idiot. "One."

"Oh. And how much are additional controllers?"

"They come with the headset," she explained. "It's one unit."

"So …"

"Additional units are $499."

Everett smiled. "I guess I'll take two."

Sure, his heart was pounding and his palms were sweating, because it was seriously bonkers to drop this much money right now. But if he was willing to spend $500 on a gift for his twin brother, why wouldn't he make the appropriate twin-sized purchase and also get one for himself?

This was what life would be like from now on. Money would be easier to make and more fun to spend. He had just given himself a chance to practice.

The clerk gave Everett the total and he tried not to swallow his tongue.

He finished paying, gripped his precious cargo, one bag per hand, then left the Gameway.

He exited the mall and stepped into the most sweltering heat of his life. His car was four rows over from where he thought he'd parked, and it felt like he might melt into the asphalt before he could get there.

He opened the car door, singeing his fingertips. It was even hotter inside — he couldn't touch the steering wheel.

He started the engine, cranked the AC, and waited for

the cabin to cool off enough to finally put the car in drive and haul ass out of the mall parking lot.

Everett pulled back onto the freeway.

And there he sat with the mall on his right, going nowhere for the next forty minutes. An accident had clogged the freeway while he'd been shopping.

He finally moved, the Aspire inching forward as its AC started to die.

Chapter Eight

THE NEW MEXICO heat was oppressive and unrelenting. Everett couldn't turn back. The only way to get where he wanted to go was through what felt like a literal hell.

But Everett wasn't a quitter. Never would be again.

So he kept his sweat-drenched hands on the wheel and his feet playing pat-a-cake with the gas and brake. He kept sipping water that was almost hot enough to make tea and telling himself that he would get where he needed to be one mile at a time.

But all that positive self-talk finally started to thin around Las Cruces.

It was boiling inside the car, and nearly all of the dashboard warning lights were on.

He drove for another twenty miles, just to prove that he wasn't afraid, but he couldn't help imagining himself dying of heat stroke by the side of the road after his bottle of water ran out. The Aspire would die if he didn't give it time to cool down soon.

He got off the highway in Las Cruces, hoping to find a Chipotle.

Instead he found a place called El Guapo's that advertised *the best two-pound burrito in New Mexico!* Lunch was delicious, but Everett ate it while worrying, suddenly having to work much harder to convince himself that even if he made it to Austin without any more problems, he might show up at the wrong time, or that maybe he wouldn't be welcome regardless of when he knocked on the door.

He needed the Ds to be wrong about this.

But what if his twin connection to Evan wasn't enough to overcome decades of separation? He wanted to curse the person who'd decided to split them up.

Back in the parking lot, he opened the passenger side door of his car and grabbed his phone from the glove compartment. The phone was hot, so he wrapped it in the bottom of his T-shirt before turning it on.

Nothing from the Ds. Nothing from Lena either, which was good — she must have taken care of the leak. But there was a text from Clara.

He'd been so busy preparing to travel that he'd forgotten to call. That's what he told himself. But there was a difference between not calling and ignoring her call. He should have at least texted to let Clara and Jimi know where he was going, and how long he expected to be gone. Then she'd have no reason to be angry if it took him a while to respond.

Now he was in a tough place. The last thing Everett wanted to do was call before connecting with his brother. He wanted a successful trip first. Clara would take it much better if Everett could tell her something about Jimi's new extended family. Once she saw him get his life together, there'd be time for them to rediscover the feelings that had brought them together in the first place. What better gift for Jimi than to give him a new family *and* heal his current one?

Everett looked forward to that conversation, playing it out in his head as he walked to the All-Mart across the street from the burrito place and bought some coolant.

But his luck gave out soon after he poured it into the radiator. After forty-five minutes back on the highway, the Aspire started in on a series of unsettling sounds. First a squealing, followed by a squeaking, different from the hissing and sizzling from when he'd first pulled over. At one point, there was definitely a sloshing, followed by a *POP!* that made him jump in his seat.

Everett didn't know what any of those sounds meant, but he was determined to keep going until he passed the Texas border into El Paso. So he ignored the warning lights and kept his eyes on the road, repeatedly assuring himself that everything would be fine.

Just forty more miles.

Twenty, ten, five.

The AC had totally stopped working and the Aspire sounded like an orchestra of danger by the time he finally pulled off the highway in El Paso a bit before seven in the evening, arriving at a mechanic's shop called The Extra Mile about five minutes later. Their sign read, *Fast service and fair prices. You'll be happy.* Everett liked all three of those promises, so he swung into the lot and parked his Aspire, wondering how many more miles he had in the beast before she finally died on him altogether.

There were two customers waiting ahead of him. But at least the shop had air conditioning inside.

"I'm sure I can help you," said Steve, the mechanic, a half hour later. "But it's getting late, and I can't promise that I'll be able to look before tomorrow."

"Tomorrow?"

"Yeah, *tomorrow.*" Steve looked at his watch, slightly less friendly.

Everett had just under six hundred miles to go. If the mechanic fixed the Aspire first thing, he could still make it to Austin in time for a special birthday dinner.

"Fine. Tomorrow it is."

Steve finished filling out the paperwork, turned it around for Everett to sign, then tore off the page and handed it over.

He would need to get a place to stay for the night. Start out early in the morning. That would be better anyway. His original plan had him driving all night to reach Austin in the early morning. But he could still arrive on his birthday — *their birthday* — and Evan would already have celebrated with his family. So the evening could be just the two of them. And Everett would surely enjoy that a lot more if he were rested.

He got out his phone, started looking for a nearby room that wouldn't break him, and ten minutes later found a place that seemed overpriced considering its three-stars, but certainly fine for one night.

But the next morning, when Everett called the shop, Steve told him that he hadn't started fixing the Aspire's AC, because apparently he'd needed to special order a part.

Everett would need to rent a car, if he was going to make it to Austin before their birthday was over.

Maybe this was an opportunity in disguise. The Aspire would be an embarrassment parked in front of Evan's beautiful home. It belonged in a trailer park, not a wealthy Austin suburb.

And first impressions were everything.

So Everett rented a stunning black Mustang.

And that made him feel like a new man. More like the man his twin brother would probably expect him to be.

Finally, his luck had turned.

· · ·

EVERETT WANDERED through the aisles of an El Paso Buc-ee's, trying not to gape. He'd seen plenty of billboards for the Texas roadside Mecca a moment after crossing the border, but he hadn't understood what the fuss was until now.

The place was the size of a Costco, with well over a hundred fuel bays. The interior was even more miraculous, considering that the place was a gas station. Buc-ee's had the country's cleanest bathrooms, just as advertised. The place sold everything from brisket burgers and burritos to lawn chairs and firewood. But their best item — a national treasure, really — were the Beaver Nuggets.

It was like eating a bag of the best cereal he'd ever had. Sweet enough to tickle his cavities. The texture was half cheese puff and half packing peanut. He couldn't get enough.

By the time he'd eaten half a bag, Everett realized he should've bought more, not just for himself, but for his new family.

A HALF HOUR LATER, he still hadn't spied a billboard for another Buc-ee's, but he did see something that made him second-guess his present wardrobe: a giant sign for a place called Redford Creek. *The place where Texas gets dressed!*

Looking down at his sweat-stained jeans, T-shirt and hoodie, Everett realized that there was nothing Texas about him at all. All three items were frayed, but until a moment ago, he hadn't thought of that as a problem. His clothes were *supposed* to look lived-in.

But he was in Texas now, and suddenly afraid of looking shabby in front of his new family.

He tried to remember what the Shepherds had been wearing in their social media posts, but he couldn't picture a single outfit. Everett had focused on how happy everyone looked, and how amazing their lives seemed.

Everett used to care about what he wore, frittering away more than a few of his paychecks at Huntington Surf & Sport, back before he owned his own business. Clara always complained that he looked like a hipster man-child, which didn't even make any sense. There was nothing "hipster" about board shorts and soft cotton tees.

"You've never even been on a surfboard," she used to argue. "I don't understand why you want the world to think you spend your life braving the waves."

But Clara never got it, no matter how many times Everett tried to explain that he was proud of his state and the culture it inspired. He wore brands like Quicksilver and Kanvis by Katin like badges of honor.

She'd wanted him to be someone more generic, dragging him to Banana Republic whenever they had a sale, forcing him to buy clothes he never felt comfortable wearing.

Everett had only gone shopping a couple of times since the divorce. Time and money were scarce these days. But really, he had also stopped caring. His last trip into Huntington Surf & Sport, the clothes had felt too expensive. He'd wondered if the style was no longer right for him. But Everett didn't know if that's how he really felt, or if that was just Clara's opinion rattling around in his head.

The more he considered it, the more self-conscious he got. And all those billboards for Redford Creek kept making things worse. He'd seen four so far, with the last one announcing that the fashion superstore was coming up in another few exits.

Everett didn't care that it was his birthday, but he did

care that it was Evan's. His twin would probably be throwing a party, and if so, everyone would probably be wearing their Texas best. His shabby T-shirt and hoodie might be fine for a campfire at a California beach party, but he'd look like a slob sitting in Evan's expensive living room.

NEXT EXIT!, the final billboard announced. *Last chance for the BEST DEALS in the place where TEXAS GETS DRESSED! A hat and boots will make a whole new YOU!*

Of course Everett knew that a hat and boots wouldn't really turn him into a different person. But it would be a nice start, especially considering the life-changing adventure he was about to embark on. Everett was going to meet his long-lost brother. *His twin brother.* He should put in the effort. Do the whole Texas thing. Prove to Evan that his twin really understood him.

He flipped on his blinker, crossed two lanes of traffic, and exited the freeway before he could change his mind. Everett hated losing even more time than he already had, but better to say adios to another half hour or so than to make a bad first impression.

The emporium, or whatever a place this big was supposed to be called, sat adjacent to the freeway, occupying what looked like a hundred acres and a parking lot the size of a small community college. Everett looked up at the giant effigies, visible from the freeway but much more imposing when seeing them up close from his parking space. A handsome couple, the man in jeans, a dignified yet colorful shirt in several shades of blue, and a wide-brimmed hat. His wife, or girlfriend, or dance partner, leaned against his shoulder, looking like a hippie cowgirl in a flowing skirt and fringed vest. She wore a matching hat, though hers was much smaller. Almost cute.

Everett started second-guessing himself after only a few

moments inside. The place was *expensive.* He'd assumed the clothes would be relatively cheap. People in this part of the country probably couldn't afford to spend as much. But most of the shirts at Redford Creek cost even more than the stuff at Huntington Surf & Sport.

The boots were *ridiculous.* And the hats even more so.

Yet, if he was going to do this thing, then boots and a hat seemed non-negotiable. He thought about maybe only getting the accessories, but after looking at himself in the full-length mirror, Everett couldn't deny that both the boots and hat looked ludicrous with his hoodie and skinny jeans.

"You look like you need some help," came a soft voice behind him.

Everett turned from the mirror, wondering how long the clerk had been standing there.

"I think I do," he admitted.

"Are you wanting something for a special occasion?" she asked.

"Sort of … I'm about to visit my brother … he lives in Austin."

"Oh, Austin's great! Awesome bars on Sixth Street. I was there a few months ago for my friend's — you know what, never mind." She laughed, pleasant and light. "I'm Amanda, how can I help you?"

She held out her hand and Everett shook it.

"I want to look like a Texan."

"You know Texans just look like everyone else, right? Especially in Austin." She laughed again. "Where are you coming from?"

"California."

"Ah. So you're just wanting to freshen up for your brother, I get it." Amanda smiled. "Can I suggest a looser-fitting pair of jeans?"

"Of course."

"And if you're going to get a hat, I'd suggest a different one. Same for the boots."

"Okay." Everett looked at the hardwood floor, embarrassed to admit this next part, but better now than while standing at the register. "I'm sort of on a budget."

"No worries," she promised.

"What about my shirt?"

"With the right jeans, boots, and a hat, you can get away with just about any shirt. Why don't we save you some money there?"

Amanda was much better at choosing an outfit for him than Clara ever was. And more efficient. Ten minutes later, Everett was looking at himself in that same mirror, with jeans that actually fit him, and somehow made his faded tee not only work, but look better than it had before. The denim fell neatly over his boots, kissing the fold so perfectly, they almost seemed worth the price. Same for the way his new hat sat neatly on his head.

He felt great — until Everett was back in the Mustang, thinking about how he'd spent almost as much on his new outfit as he had on the gaming system. And he still had to pay for the rented Mustang.

Worse, revenue at Joe's would likely be down while he was away. Lena was competent, but she was no marketer. And he'd promised her a raise. No, *two* raises. What had he been thinking?

His stomach ached again. He should be excited about his new life, not worried about old problems. At least he wouldn't have to spend any money in Austin. Surely Evan would be happy to put his twin brother up in that fancy house of his.

He stopped at a Buc-ee's in Bastrop and bought himself a sandwich and a soda. Loaded up on Beaver

Nuggets. Strengthened his resolve in the country's cleanest bathrooms.

He checked his phone while gassing up and saw another two messages from Clara. She'd be furious by now, which made it even more important that he have some good news before calling her back.

It wouldn't be long now.

Chapter Nine

EVERETT WAS PARKED in front of Evan's house in Westlake, but he couldn't make himself get out of the car. Now just moments away from meeting his twin brother, the gravity of it all was too much.

He'd kept his promise and not looked at Evan's or his family's social media profiles even once during his two-day trip. But now, it felt like he had no other choice.

He wasn't even killing time, at least not exactly. He was looking through Evan's LiveLyfe profile with purpose. He had been picturing his introduction — or visualizing it, as Clara would say. But no matter how hard he imagined the exchange, Everett couldn't conjure the perfect opening line. Everything sounded stupid as soon as he said it out loud. He deserved a cinematic moment, an unforgettable reunion between long-lost brothers. But every line felt like it came from the wrong genre of film.

He set his phone on the passenger seat and looked back at his brother's home with a sigh that tried hard not to be envious. The place was much more impressive in person, owning its corner with a regal profile and stunning landscaping. Almost palatial. Three cars occupied the long driveway: a pair of Teslas (one black and the other white), parked with a cherry red Prius right in between them.

Evan pulled away from the curb. No reason he couldn't take a little tour of the neighborhood for inspiration. The more he saw himself fitting into a place like this, the more confident he'd feel about knocking on his brother's door.

The plots were spacious, and seemed neatly divided between older homes — maybe from the 60s or 70s — and larger, more impressive custom builds.

His favorite was a three-story beauty nested high on a rise that made the property look like a resort. He made the mistake of looking it up RealEstated, and couldn't believe that the sprawling hill country estate had a price tag of just $1.7 million. A property that size and stature in California would cost three or four times as much, unless there had been a massacre inside it.

As he parked in front of Evan's house again, he felt more intimidated than ever.

You belong here.

Evan will be so excited to meet you.

This is the beginning of the best part of your life.

Everett pictured the surprise and gratitude on Evan's face, and that was enough to get him opening the Mustang door.

But then he closed it again. And reached for his phone.

He wanted to check Evan's LiveLyfe profile once more, see if there were pics of the party he was about to walk into. But apparently Evan hadn't felt like sharing that part of his life with the world, and neither had Klair.

But he did see three new texts from Clara, and one missed call.

Where are you?

Why haven't you texted me back?

Then, to his surprise: *Is everything okay? I'm starting to worry.*

Apparently she'd contacted the Ds as well, because their voicemails sounded even more distressed.

This was making things worse. *Focus, Everett.*

He imagined holding a bag of Beaver Nuggets in one hand, and his Gameway bags in the other as he tried out entrance lines.

Happy birthday!

Did you think I would just show up to meet my long-lost twin brother without bringing some gifts?

And the best one so far: *I couldn't decide between a sweet Texas delicacy, a bleeding-edge video game system, or a long-lost twin — so I decided to bring all three!*

LiveLyfe dinged. Finally, a post. From Klair rather than Evan.

Happy birthday to the most amazing man in the world!

Klair's words were centered underneath the kind of photo that Everett had always longed to be in. Evan in the center, his beaming wife and children close around him, plus an older couple who didn't look related. His adoptive parents? Or Klair's?

It didn't matter. Now Everett knew that the party was family only.

Soon to be *his* family.

He donned his hat, checked the way his cuffs were kissing his boots, then grabbed the Beaver Nuggets and the Gameway bags and headed for the front door. He really should have had the systems wrapped, and dammit, he hadn't even thought to get a card.

But he was the real gift, wasn't he?

Everett rang the doorbell, waited twenty seconds, then rang it again.

Still nothing. Not even after another two minutes and three long knocks.

He didn't want to think the worst, but Everett started wondering if maybe he was being ignored. If maybe they were all on the other side of the door, laughing at him.

The Beaver Nuggets felt awkward in his hand, and the Gameway bags were getting heavy.

Maybe he should just go ahead and make the call. He had Evan's number from the background check. He should have had it programmed into his phone and ready to go, but it felt like a jinx to play for failure. It would be a shame to lose out on the cinematic moment of that door opening to twin brothers seeing each other for the very first time. Especially after a cross-country drive. But Everett didn't know what else to do.

Why weren't they answering their door?

Could that Livelyfe photo have been taken in the elderly couple's home instead if this one?

Everett set down the Gameway bags, dropped the Beaver Nuggets into one of them, then took out his phone and searched for Evan's number.

The door opened and Everett looked up.

His brother. No longer a picture, now in the flesh.

Evan looked back at him, but it was a broken mirror moment.

And the shards were already falling. This was nothing at all like he had imagined.

His mind went blank.

Evan stared at him in shock.

Everett remained paralyzed on the doorstep for the longest five, six, seven seconds of his life.

"Happy birthday!" he finally blurted.

"Thanks?" Evan still looked baffled.

"Did I get the day wrong?" Everett laughed nervously.

"No … it's my birthday."

"I'm Everett Alvarez. Your twin brother from California."

"I can see that. At least the twin part." Evan stood back from the door, finally loosening up. "Look, I'm sorry. Happy birthday to you, too. This is just such a surprise."

"Isn't it great?" A cumbersome smile. "I drove all the way from California."

"Without even calling?" Evan looked baffled, when he should have looked honored. He nodded toward the Mustang. "Is that yours?"

Everett could hear the Ds in his head, warning him that he was being foolish. This was all going so very wrong.

"I'm sorry. I don't mean to intrude. I just found out I had a brother a few days ago, and since it was my — I mean *our* birthday week, I thought it would be fun to surprise you. But now I realize that I should have called first."

After another moment's hesitation, Evan opened the door all the way and said, "Happy birthday. Would you like to come in and meet my family?"

Not *our family*, but still a great start.

"Yes, please."

Evan closed the door behind them and pointed at Everett's boots. "We don't wear our shoes in the house, so if you wouldn't mind …"

"Oh, of course." Everett suddenly felt ridiculous. He looked like he was wearing a cowboy costume, while Evan looked trendy in high-end jogging pants, T-shirt and hoodie — the look that everyone constantly told Everett he was too old for.

Evan waited for Everett to get his idiotic boots off, then walked away, expecting his brother to follow.

When Everett entered the laughter-filled living room, everyone froze.

Gaped at him.

Traded glances.

Then Harmony said, "You look like my dad, except sad and fat."

Chapter Ten

EVERETT LAUGHED to prove that he didn't mind being referred to as the sadder and fatter version of his twin brother.

"Hey everybody," he waved, "I'm Everett Alvarez, Evan's twin."

Klair stole a glance at her husband. Evan shrugged with a *hell if I know?* expression.

Clearly it was on Everett to take charge.

"I've come from California bearing gifts." He raised each of his hands yet again.

"You can set those over there." Another smile from Klair. She pointed toward the kitchen island where Everett could see a scattering of other wrapped presents.

"Thanks." He shuffled over to the counter and set them down while everyone watched him.

"Everett drove here from California," Evan said.

"Your home is beautiful," Everett said, trying to melt the tension without appearing to case the place.

"Thanks," Klair replied with a tired smile. "Sometimes it feels like a full-time job keeping up with the place."

"I'm sure it is," said the older woman. "Unless Evan's finally learned to pick up after himself."

Should Everett defend his brother, and possibly offend his new … aunt?

He thought of his apartment back home as he took in the polished marble and hardwood floors. Even at its cleanest, his place was still trash. He was grateful that Evan hadn't been the one to seek him out.

But he'd be able to afford something better soon.

"It's very nice to meet you." Klair turned to her husband. "Can you please help me with something in the kitchen?"

"Of course," Evan said.

Then he was gone and Everett was alone with Evan's family. They'd be his family too soon enough, but right now they all felt like the strangers they were.

"I'm William, and this is my wife, Dorothy." The older gentleman offered his hand. "You can call me Bill."

"We're Evan's adopted parents," Dorothy explained.

Everett shook Bill's hand, then Dorothy's, before turning to the children. "And you must be Harmony and Jazz."

"Hey," Harmony said, seeming completely uninterested in her father's twin brother.

"Hey," Jazz echoed, with what sounded like a light note of curiosity.

Bill asked, "That must have been a strange experience, finding out that you had a twin brother."

"It was," Everett said, but then for some reason he couldn't just leave it at that. "I guess I've always known that I had one … or something."

"What was your family like growing up?" Dorothy asked.

What could he tell them that wouldn't make him sound like a total loser?

"A really nice couple. They adopted me when they found out they couldn't have any more children."

"Oh?" Dorothy said. "How many siblings do you have?"

"And what's the age difference?" Bill added.

"Marco was ten and Roberto was twelve when I was a baby."

"Bless your sweet mother!" Dorothy laughed. "How did your brothers feel about your arrival?"

Everett laughed, mostly to make himself feel less alone. "Mixed feelings, I guess."

"Are you boys close to your parents?"

Everett wasn't expecting the surge of that followed Dorothy's question. Here he was, talking to the mother he could have had, just days after losing the mother offered by fate. And he would've given anything to trade Dorothy for another minute with the woman who'd raised him.

Coming here had been a mistake.

"Our dad died a few years ago, and our mom passed just last week, so the last time I saw them was at the funeral."

"Oh …" Dorothy touched her face. "I'm so sorry to hear that."

"It's okay. She was … at least she's not suffering now."

Thankfully, Evan and Klair returned, giving Everett a chance to change the subject.

"I'm sorry I didn't call ahead. Maybe I should—"

"Nonsense." Evan clapped his shoulder and offered him a much more genuine smile than before. "You're my brother."

Then Evan really surprised Everett by pulling him into a hug.

"You have a wonderful family," Everett said when they parted.

"Do you want to go outside and fly my drone with me later?" Jazz asked.

"I would love that!" The smile probably looked stupid on his face, but Everett didn't even care.

"Just … please … no more …" Klair couldn't finish, or really even start her sentence.

"I won't, Mom." Jazz was clearly embarrassed by his mother's half-thought. He turned to Everett and waved. "See you later."

"Are you coming back for presents and cake?" Klair asked.

"Half an hour?" Jazz said.

"Sure."

Harmony frowned. "Why does he get to go?"

Evan and Klair together: "*Harmony*."

"Whatever. Mind if I go and make sure the ice cream is frozen?" Then she sauntered off toward the kitchen without waiting for an answer.

"Ev—" Klair started.

"Yes?" both brothers responded in unison.

"Sorry." She touched her husband's arm. "I meant *Evan*."

Everett flushed. Of course she did. Why would she be talking to a brother-in-law she'd known for less than ten minutes?

"Well, this is going to get sticky," Dorothy said.

Bill suggested, "Why don't we call you Rhett?"

Klair nodded. "Rhett it is."

Except that Everett really hated that idea.

Evan turned to Klair. "What were you going to say?"

"I was going to suggest that you make your brother a drink."

"Oh. Sure thing." Back to Everett. "You have a favorite?"

"Margaritas, usually. But what do you suggest?"

"I suggest that you follow me." Evan smiled, then led his brother to the bar. "Besides driving across country, how do you most like to celebrate your birthday: big party with lots of friends, or an intimate gathering with only a few?"

"Intimate gathering for sure."

"You're out with friends and someone orders drinks for the group. It's your turn and you only have three seconds to think. Margaritas are off the menu — what do you order?"

"A shot of something," Everett said.

"You have a ton of work to do. Procrastinate or lick the frog?"

"Lick the frog?"

"Procrastinate or get it done?"

"Get it done!" Because Everett didn't want to admit the other.

"Do you prefer savory or sweet?" Evan asked.

"Sweet."

"Are you more likely to take a nap or go to the gym?"

That one was embarrassing. Not just because the answer was obvious by looking at him. If he and his brother both took their shirts off, Everett might cry.

"Take a nap," he admitted.

"Burger or seafood?"

"Burger."

"What are you most likely to order on a date?"

"This is a lot of questions," Everett said.

"Good news, this is the last one. After you answer, I'll know your perfect drink."

"Depends on what my date orders, but I guess I would want something I can sip."

Evan smiled as he pulled down a glass from the shelf. "Just what I thought."

"So what's my drink?"

"I suggest a whiskey neat."

"You mean … like a shot?" Everett asked.

"No, not a shot." Evan shook his head, giving Everett what felt like an admonishing look while grabbing a bottle of Artemis Tull from the bar.

"I don't think I like whiskey."

"Have you ever tried it?" Evan asked.

"I've had a—"

"Without adding anything to it?"

"No."

Evan finished pouring the whiskey, then gave it to Everett. "Neat means no frills, not even rocks. You can sip the alcohol slowly enough to appreciate it. You're not trying to get drunk … you're savoring the drink's complex flavors."

Everett placed the glass underneath his nose and took a whiff. He didn't hate it, but he didn't love it either. "How do you know I'll like this?"

"Because it's my favorite." Evan grinned and poured a glass for himself, which he raised it in a toast. "We are twins, aren't we?"

Glasses clinked and Everett felt a spark of something true and wonderful.

This was what he'd been waiting an entire lifetime to feel.

A half hour passed in a flash as he told Evan a sanitized version of his life story, focusing on the similarities between them: the sibling rivalry without the bullying, Mom's lessons in the kitchen without Dad's contempt, his son's birth and the divorce he pretended had been amicable. Everett's description of Java Joe's was rosier than the café deserved, even when it was at its newest and most successful. The rest could come later, once Evan knew his brother better.

Or maybe never — now that his life was turning around, maybe he could just share his successes going forward.

He expected Evan to brag about his own personal triumphs, but when Everett asked about Señor Sushi and Tequila Mockingbird, his brother changed the subject.

So he tried something easier. "How do you like living in Texas?"

"Austin or Texas?"

"What's the difference?" Austin was *in* Texas.

"It's different." Evan laughed.

"That's not very specific."

Evan shrugged. "Well, let's see … some people say we're a blue dot in a red state, and others say the same thing by calling us 'weird.' We're the live music capital of the world."

"I heard that!"

"We have our own culture. People here really care about food and technology, the environment and—"

"Sounds like California," Everett said after a sip.

"But without the Californians." Evan laughed.

So did Everett, but he wasn't sure if that was an insult.

"Plus, it's cheaper to live here, right?" Everett still couldn't stop thinking about that 1.7-million-dollar mansion just two blocks away."

"It's not San Antonio cheap, but compared to LA or New York or Boston, it's not even close. But … it is getting more expensive all the time."

"Oh yeah?" Narrow the gap in housing costs, and California might look more attractive.

"Great schools where we live, especially for the money, but our house value has doubled since we moved in."

"How long ago was that?"

"Ten years. But we've also done a lot of work. Added the pool, and our guest house out back."

And it all looked brochure-handsome. Surely he'd be able to sell it for a huge profit, which would make it easier to get into a great place in Las Orillas, once Evan got a taste for California.

"Traffic keeps getting worse," Evan said. "But it's still not as bad as some of the concrete jungles in Texas. No natural disasters like all your fires and earthquakes."

"They're not *mine*," Everett laughed, and took a sip of his very delicious whiskey.

"Fair enough. I met Klair like a million years ago, but from what I understand, the dating scene in this city is terrific." Evan shrugged. "It's a great place to live."

"Have you been in Austin all your life?"

"My parents moved us here when I was ten."

"*Us?*"

"My older sister, Samantha. She's in Kenya right now."

"Kenya? What's she doing there?"

"Building roads," Evan said.

"Oh. Are you close?"

"Too close." Evan laughed. "She's always telling me what to do."

"Was your sister adopted too?"

"Three years before me, and she was four when I was only a baby. I'll never catch up — she still thinks I don't know anything."

Everett couldn't help feeling a little hurt. Bill and Dorothy had wanted two children, but somehow not him?

Why was Evan wanted by everyone while Everett was wanted by no one?

"Am I interrupting?" Klair asked.

"Cake time?" Evan said.

"Cake time," Klair repeated with a nod.

Evan gave his brother a glance: *We'll finish this later.*

Of course Everett was disappointed, but they'd bond later. Now that Evan had accepted him, surely the rest of his family would too.

They followed Klair to the kitchen counter, where a cake now sat artfully centered amid all those presents. The cake looked like a wet burrito, with raspberry puree as ranchero sauce drizzled across the top and onto the plate below. A proud dollop of whipped instead of sour cream, and what Everett guessed was a large scoop of pistachio ice cream in place of guacamole. His mouth watered, imagining the sweet layers inside that cakey burrito.

"We were going to put forty candles in it," Harmony announced, "but we didn't want to burn the house down."

Evan grunted. "Sure didn't see that one coming."

"I'm surprised you can even remember what a joke is at your age," said Jazz.

Everett laughed, feeling younger than ever. But Evan shot him a grumpy look before pasting on a smile for his family

"Hurry, there's ice cream." Klair lit the candles and stepped away from the cake. "Three ... two ... one ..."

Then the room was singing.

But it stung when Evan's name was the only one harmonized. And it stung a little more when Everett's brother blew out the candles without inviting him to blow too. It would've been so easy to include him, knowing that it was his birthday too — but Klair was already cutting the cake.

Habit, he told himself. They weren't used to him yet. By Christmas, he'd be a member of the family.

"What did you wish for?" Jazz asked his father.

"I've never told you that before," Evan shook his head, "and turning forty isn't about to change my MO."

"Then tell us what you're thinking, now that you're over the hill." Klair took his arm with a smile.

"Forty is the new thirty, and I don't know why you're always on me about being older, since you're only a year behind me."

"Because I will *always* be a year behind you, and therefore *never* as old as you."

"You're both ancient," Harmony muttered, but with a smile.

Everett eyed the pile of gifts and wished for another whiskey to sip while hiding his discomfort. He hadn't realized that showing up unannounced meant he'd be celebrating his twin's birthday without anyone celebrating his.

At least at home, the Ds would have made a big deal about the day and invited him over to play games all evening. Jessa would've made tacos and bought an ice cream cake.

As soon as Bill and Dorothy left, Everett would suggest that they break in those gaming consoles.

"Thanks, guys. For all of this." Evan smiled. "Jokes aside, I have no fear of growing older. I was raised by remarkable parents who made sure I always felt loved. I have a gorgeous, supportive wife who I've loved for nearly half of my life now. And two remarkable children who I'm so incredibly proud of."

Evan looked at everyone before finishing, including Everett. "I'm proud of everything I've done in my first forty years, and even prouder to know that I'm just getting started." He looked down at the burrito cake. "Can we start eating, or are we opening presents first?"

It was hard not to feel envious, but Everett shut that part of himself off. He shouldn't be seeing everything around him as "the life he never had" when it was so clearly "the life he could still achieve." But he suddenly felt thirty pounds too heavy and ten years behind his older brother, instead of the few seconds their birth certificates claimed.

He forced himself to smile while Evan opened his presents, feeling more and more out of place. He was used to being a third wheel. Or an unwanted unicycle lying unloved in the corner. But right now he felt like that unicycle getting dragged behind the train on its way to an entirely different circus.

Evan unwrapped a set of drinking glasses and some sort of fitness tracker.

The glasses didn't seem all that special, but Evan's expression was almost awed as he seemed to weigh them, moving the set with affection from one hand to the other.

"These are gorgeous," Evan said in admiration.

Bill gave his adopted son an appreciative nod. "A whiskey is only as refined as the glass it's served in."

Evan made a fuss over the fitness tracker too, which apparently recorded a lot more than steps.

Harmony gave him a pair of sunglasses, and Jazz gave him a homemade mug that read *World's Greatest Dad*.

Evan was having the most boring birthday ever.

Two boxes left, both from Klair, though she snatched the smaller one away, quickly and with obvious embarrassment. "Sorry, that one's not supposed to be there."

"What is it?" Jazz asked.

"Something gross," Harmony said.

"It's for your father." Klair put the smaller box into a drawer in the sideboard.

The bigger box was a new espresso maker. Silver and

black, better than the secondhand monstrosity that Everett had scrounged for Java Joe's.

"I know you've been wanting a new one," Klair said.

"It's perfect." Evan pulled the espresso maker out of its box, set it gently on the counter, and began to study it with an appreciative gaze. "I love it."

"This man *adores* his coffee," Klair explained to Everett. "And our old maker's been on the fritz for a while."

"Someone used milk instead of water," Jazz said, with a sideways glance at his sister.

"This one comes with a frothing pitcher, a tamping tool, and a measuring spoon."

"I think they all do, Mom." Harmony looked like she was dying to roll her eyes.

Klair laughed. "Well, they're better in this model."

"Your mother's right." Evan gave her a kiss. "Thank you for everything."

"Are those from you, dear?" Dorothy asked Everett, gesturing to the Gameway bags still sitting on the table.

"Oh yeah, they're nothing."

"It's not nothing," Evan said, looking to Jazz. "It's two Infinite Fidelity units."

"REALLY?" Everett had never seen a happier child. "I thought you said we couldn't get that yet."

"I did." Evan tousled his hair. "But it looks like I was wrong."

Jazz ran over to the bags and started digging for treasure.

"What's this?" Evan asked, pulling out a bag of Beaver Nuggets.

"They're from Buc-ee's," Klair explained, almost apologetically.

Cake was served and quietly eaten, then the tiny crowd dispersed. Jazz went back to the pair of Infinite Fidelity units and began to unbox them. Everett tried to make small talk with Bill and Dorothy, but when even that felt like too much heavy lifting, he walked over and attempted to engage Harmony in a friendly exchange. She somehow managed to make him feel older, younger, and dumber than anyone else.

After Bill and Dorothy bid their farewells, Klair and Evan retreated to a corner of the kitchen to whisper. Probably about Everett, or maybe about whatever was in Evan's little box. Either way, he should get going. He just needed five minutes to talk with his brother first.

Everett circled the living room, looking at pictures on the mantle displaying the life he could've had. Jealousy swelled, worse than before.

Not the life he *could* have had, the life he *should* have had.

The life he didn't have, because Bill and Dorothy hadn't wanted him.

Was it chance that they had chosen Evan over him, or had they sensed a difference between the boys that made Evan a better fit for this life?

Did Evan have something that Everett had lacked from the start?

How could that be, when they were identical twins?

Everett reminded himself that this was his family too. They just had to get used to each other. He would prove that he was just as good as Evan. Make them see what a mistake they'd made in choosing one twin while abandoning the other.

But it still wouldn't make up for everything Everett had missed out on in life by being second.

Chapter Eleven

Klair finally sent the children upstairs, with instructions to get ready for bed. Then she turned to their guest.

"It was really good meeting you, Rhett." She gave him an awkward hug. "I'm sure we'll be seeing each other again."

The word *soon* was conspicuously missing from the end of her sentence.

"I was hoping for a few minutes alone with my brother?" Everett didn't need a lot, just enough to feel something there. He could come back tomorrow, or even the day after that. It wasn't fair how he had surprised them. Definitely not his smartest move. Fair enough, lesson learned.

"Oh, of course." A spot of color on her pale cheeks. "Don't keep him too long."

She turned to her husband with what he imagined as *hurry up* in her eyes, then went upstairs herself.

Finally, a moment alone.

But before he could thank Evan for his hospitality, Evan asked, "So, where are you staying?"

"Oh … um …" That caught Everett off guard, even though he should have been fully prepared. "I know this is really stupid, but I was just so excited about driving out here and meeting … well, all of you guys … I didn't stop to book anything." He offered Evan a brittle, awkward laugh. "One thing at a time, I guess."

Evan stared at him, as if chewing on a thought.

"How long are you planning on staying in Austin?"

Everett didn't know how to respond. His actual answer was, *As long as you'll have me.*

But in truth, if Everett was paying for his own room, then he couldn't really afford to stay a day. He needed to get back to El Paso and return the Mustang, pay for the work on his Aspire, then drive that piece of shit all the way back to California.

That reminded him of the unanswered texts and voice-mail from Clara, plus the two messages from Devon and Derek that he still hadn't answered.

"My only plan was to meet my brother … I just found out that you existed and got carried away. I'm really sorry about that … I don't want to impose at all." Everett straightened his shoulders. "I can be away from the restaurant for about a week — you know how it is — but I can also leave in the morning … if that's better for you and everyone else."

"Come on." Evan clapped him on the shoulder, if not like a brother then at least like a buddy. "You can stay in the guest house if it's just one night."

"Really?"

"Really. That's what it's for. Follow me."

His time was expiring. Klair was waiting for Evan upstairs. Long lost brother or not, Everett had a good idea what he was delaying.

If he had something to say, then he needed to say it.

Now, before their walk was over. Any second … they were already past the pool, a few feet away from the guest house. He needed an opening line, but his head was even emptier than his checking account.

Evan stopped at the guest house and opened the door. "After you."

"Thanks." Everett stepped past his brother and looked around the living room, which was bigger than his entire apartment. And a thousand times nicer.

But for Evan, this was all *extra.* Another little home in his back yard, *just in case.*

How could Everett be so jealous of the man he'd been waiting his entire life to meet?

Evan was dying to get out of there, Everett could see it in his eyes and the way he hovered in the open doorway, seemingly waiting for permission to go.

Everett had to remind himself that Evan hadn't asked for any of this. While he'd had several days to think about this meeting, his brother had awoken this morning without any idea that he had a twin who would appear without warning at his party.

Evan would rest his head on a soft pillow beside his beautiful wife while Everett would spend the next several hours tossing and turning in the guest house alone. At least he wasn't looking for a room at La Quinta. He should be grateful that Evan hadn't kicked him out.

"You need anything else?" Evan asked.

"No, I'm good." But then he shook his head. "Actually, I was really hoping we could stay up and talk a little. Maybe get to know one another."

Evan sighed with what sounded like relief. Like maybe he'd been expecting the request and could put it to bed. "I understand, and I'm sorry, but it's been a long—"

"Maybe in the morning?"

"There's a lot to do at the restaurant. I'm an early to bed, early to rise kind of guy."

"Me too. We move a lot of coffee in my restaurant. So, early hours."

"Then you understand," Evan said.

"Well, yeah, under normal circumstances. But it's not every day you meet your long-lost twin."

"I know. And I'm sorry." Evan's face softened. "I do get where you're coming from, and I swear this isn't personal. But I just found out that you'd be here a few hours ago, after my day and night were already planned."

"I understand." And he did, no matter how much it hurt.

"It's been a long day, and tomorrow promises to be even longer. But I promise, we'll figure out a time to catch up, okay?"

"Cool," Everett agreed with a smile.

Evan surprised him with a hug. "Thanks for driving all this way."

"Thanks for having me."

Evan walked to the door, opened it, then turned back before leaving. "Happy birthday."

"Happy birthday!"

The door closed, but Everett could still feel his smile.

He turned on the TV, then went to pour himself a drink at the small bar. Whiskey, neat. He tipped it back and gulped it like a shot, before setting the bottle of whiskey back on the counter and pushing his empty glass back toward the ledge. Then he turned off the TV, plugged in his phone, and set an alarm for six in the morning.

Drinking right now was dumb, and watching TV was even dumber.

He needed to sleep, so he could wake up fresh and early to talk with Evan first thing.

Then maybe he could be a part of his brother's life.

Everett left the guest house, lost a couple of minutes trying to figure out the gate, grabbed his suitcase from the trunk of his rented Mustang, then brought it back inside to leave it on the guest house floor without doing anything else.

He got undressed, to hell with brushing his teeth, then collapsed on a queen-sized mattress that was better than the one he had at home in every conceivable way.

Moments later he was falling asleep, thinking about all the many ways tomorrow could go right.

If it didn't go terribly, terribly wrong.

Chapter Twelve

Everett's alarm went off at exactly six in the morning.

The sound of the overlapping chimes was peaceful, more a lullaby than a sonic charge to get him out of the bed. Everett had been dreaming he was on a boat, bobbing up and down in a mostly calm sea as little waves licked at the hull.

Until he remembered his plan to talk to Evan and shot straight up in bed, half-panicked.

He rolled out of bed, fumbled for his phone, finding it only after remembering that he'd left it plugged in across the room. He killed the alarm, looked at the screen, saw that it was 6:16 and cursed himself.

It's not too late, you can do this, he told himself, peeling off his clothes on the way into the bathroom. He turned on the shower and jumped under the stream without waiting for his water to get hot. No time for that, he barely had a moment to lather the shampoo. His hair, face, and body were all washed by the time the water started scalding him.

He got out, ran a towel over his body, then went to his suitcase and dug for a change of clothes, casting a dirty glance at both his cowboy hat and boots. He put on yesterday's jeans, which were much better than the skinnies, and a gray tee with the words *Pot Head* beneath a steaming pot of coffee.

He slipped into his hoodie, put on his shoes, then walked from the guest house to his brother's back door, knocking softly. When no one answered, Everett worried that he might have already blown it.

He knocked again, slightly harder, pissed at himself for sleeping through that first quarter hour of his alarm. Now it was 6:29, and Evan might already be gone.

He knocked a third time, louder than he meant to. Still no answer. So he circled around to the front of the house.

The black Tesla was gone. *Dammit.*

How early did Evan get up?

Was it possibly he'd left earlier than normal to avoid Everett?

He considered getting in the car and driving to Señor Sushi. He could offer to help his brother out in the kitchen. They were both chefs, after all. Cooking together would be fun, and maybe Everett could even teach Evan a thing or two. Dorothy might've been a loving mother, but she couldn't possibly be as good a cook as Mom.

But he could already hear the Ds telling him not to push it. He'd shown up unannounced at Evan's birthday party. It might be too much to show up at his restaurant unannounced, too. It would be so much better to be invited.

He'd talk to Evan tonight, drop a hint.

For today, he might as well relax. Make himself a hearty breakfast from the guest house's fully-stocked fridge. Mom had always served him the best food in the world. Chilaquiles with salsa verde. A pork tamale topped with a fried egg and drizzled in Aunt Beatriz' homemade hot sauce. Corn pancakes spiced with cinnamon, drizzled with sweet cajeta and sprinkled with chopped pecans.

Remembering her bustling around their cramped kitchen made him tear up.

He looked up and down the street, as if that could tell him anything, then sighed in defeat and turned back around to head inside the guest house.

He opened a window to the city by turning on the local news, then went and took inventory in the fridge. It appeared recently stocked, and surely just for him. When had they done that? He saw bacon, sausage, and several kinds of cheese, eggs — Everett wouldn't be able to make any of Mom's recipes, but he could make an amazing omelette.

But eyeing all his options, he suddenly didn't feel like cooking at all, overwhelmed by a wave of melancholy. Even with all of Mom's recipes, he would never cook with her again.

He closed the fridge and plopped onto the couch and actually watched the TV.

Maybe that wasn't such a good idea. He had been hoping for a glimpse into Austin, but even this early in the morning Everett was only seeing the same old stories about war and inequality, oppression and pollution, crime and punishment, power and abuse. He had no idea if the world was really getting worse, but it sure felt like it was.

A half hour later, he went to try the back door of the main house yet again. This time, three soft knocks earned him an answer.

"Everett ... good morning." Klair looked like she'd been awake for all of five minutes.

"Good morning ..." His moment was finally here, but he didn't know how to use it. "I'm guessing Evan already went into work?"

"Um … yeah. He's usually out of here by 5:00, 5:30 at the latest."

"Oh."

"He has a lot to do right now, keeping the old restaurant running while preparing to open the new one. But I can't even blame it on that." She shrugged. "Evan's been up and out of here ahead of the sun for years."

"That's the restaurant business for you," Everett said, thinking of Lena with a stab of guilt for all those mornings she opened for him.

"Right."

Klair's smile hung on her face like an obligation. Everett understood; it wasn't like *she* was his twin. And he was in her space, early in the morning. Still … would it kill her to invite him inside?

"Will he be gone all day?" Everett asked.

"He's always gone all day."

After several more seconds of awkward silence, Klair finally got the hint and opened the door.

"You're welcome to sit around while I prep lunches. It's not exciting, but—"

"That would be great."

Everett followed her into the kitchen, then sat at the large island where they had opened presents the night before. What looked like a random assembly of ingredients littered the counter.

"What are you making?" Everett asked, hoping the question would warm her up.

"Depends on who it's for," Klair said, sounding as tired as she looked. "Pesto zucchini for Harmony, turkey burger kabobs for Jazz. The only thing they have in common is that neither one eats gluten."

"Once they're off to school, then you can relax?"

"Then I've got a meeting with our tour manager. And a rehearsal this afternoon."

It never occurred to Everett that she would be in a hurry to get out of the house too. Clara worked her rehearsals around Jimi's schedule, often hosting the band in her tiny garage.

Because Everett was always too busy at the café to take Jimi during the week.

"What's in a burger kabob?" he asked, to distract himself from the twinge of guilt.

Klair pointed at the prep bowls of ingredients as she explained. "I made the turkey meatballs yesterday. Everything else is straight from the fridge. I cut the cheese into little squares, and put it on a toothpick with a little wedge of lettuce, a piece of pickle, and a cherry tomato. *Boom*, turkey burger kabob."

"Is there anything I can do to help out?" Everett asked.

She shook her head. "The hard part's all done. Now it's just assembly. I try to prep as much as I can the day before."

"In that case, have you eaten breakfast?" Maybe he could warm her up by cooking for her. That was how he'd won Clara over. With gourmet pasta and his secret weapon: Mom's oatmeal raisin cookie recipe. Tinged with a hint of cardamom and orange, in addition to the usual cinnamon and vanilla, they were orgasmic hot out of the oven, especially when paired with a scoop of vanilla ice cream. Clara had begged to take a few home the morning after their first date; he'd always wondered if she'd have said yes to the second date if he hadn't offered to let her take the whole batch.

"The fridge in the guest house is fully stocked. If you're hungry, make yourself something. You have a restaurant, right?"

"I do." That one wasn't *really* a lie.

"There's even some chicken jalapeño sausage from Central Market. It'll kick you in your teeth."

"What's Central Market? And do I want to get kicked in my teeth?"

"Do you like spicy?"

"I love spicy!"

"Then yes, you want to get kicked in your teeth. Central Market is the bougie Austin grocery store that has things like jalapeño chicken sausage. Better than Whole Foods."

"What if I made something for the both of us? You don't want to go off to your meetings hungry."

"I don't have a lot of time—"

"Ten minutes. I'll make a scrambler, sausage and eggs."

She hesitated, then said, "There's more of that sausage in here."

While Klair finished assembling the kids' lunches, Everett worked fast, adding some chopped onion and shredded cheddar he'd found in the fridge to the scrambled eggs and sausage.

"Morning, Mom!" Harmony yelled as she exploded into the kitchen.

"You're late." Klair sealed up the lunch containers and wiped her hands on a kitchen towel.

"I'm earlier than Jazz."

"I'm right here!" Jazz announced, running into the kitchen a beat behind his sister.

Harmony looked at Everett. "You're still here."

"Morning to you both." Everett gave them his best smile. *Uncle Everett is happy to see you, kids.*

"Is that for us?" Harmony asked.

But before he could offer to make more, Klair answered. "You know the rules."

Harmony groaned, but Jazz was already digging through the pantry.

"Here." He tossed something to Harmony, but Everett couldn't see what it was.

"Great," Harmony said.

Klair turned to Everett. "That girl has no idea how spoiled she is."

"I'm right here, Mom."

"I'm pretty sure she said that for your benefit," Jazz explained.

"You're late," Klair reminded them both.

Quick kisses and hugs, then Harmony and Jazz were out the door.

Everett and Klair were alone again.

"What's 'the rule'?" he asked.

"If they're up early, I'll make them breakfast. An omelette, a smoothie, oatmeal, whatever. But they can't come down last minute and ask me to drop everything."

She grabbed a plate from a nearby cabinet, plucked a fork from the drawer beneath it, and helped herself to some of the scrambler. Once she'd put the first bite in her mouth, she smiled and made a happy humming noise.

And Everett realized that was the first thing he'd cooked since—

"Are you planning to check out the city?" Klair asked.

He'd hoped to get to know her. He would be happy to help her with whatever she needed. Meal prep for tonight, lunch prep for tomorrow. Housework, even. Anything to help her get comfortable with his presence, so that she'd push Evan to let him stay instead of pushing to get rid of him.

But if she was anything like Clara, she'd resent having him hanging around, even if he was trying to help.

"No plans yet." Everett dished the rest of the scrambler

onto a plate for himself. "I was listening to some of your music the other day. Really great stuff. My favorite song was 'Polished Pebbles.'"

"Thanks."

Everett expected more in the aftermath of his compliment, but instead, she asked, "There are a lot of great trails in Austin, if you like to hike."

Everett definitely didn't want to go hiking. "So, how did you guys meet? You and Evan, I mean."

"It was sophomore year of college."

"You were both at UT?"

"Yep."

There had to be mountains more to that story, but Klair clearly wasn't interested in climbing any of it. She needed time to get used to him — time he couldn't afford. The clock was ticking on his bank account.

"So, Rhett …" she started.

He looked up, ignoring her use of the new name that he already hated.

"How about I give you a list of some great things to do in Austin, then you can go ahead and get started on your day?"

That way I can get started on mine, she didn't need to add.

"What do you like?" she asked.

"Which of the restaurants will Evan be at today?"

She shook her head, looking … *concerned?* "I don't think that's a good idea."

"What's not a good idea?"

"When Evan's working, you don't want to interrupt him. It's like he's in another world."

"Oh, I get it, I'm the same way in the kitchen." He finished the last of his scrambler. "I'd only drop by to say *hi.*"

"*Hi* is an interruption. Oh my God — don't ever text him *hi* and then nothing else. He'll cook you for dinner."

"Got it. Don't go near the restaurants."

"He'll be at Señor until after the dinner rush. But seriously, don't go there."

"Where would you suggest going to chill out?"

"Did you bring any of that California weed with you?"

"No. Sorry." Clearly an oversight. That would have been better than Beaver Nuggets for sure.

"Fuck," Klair said.

Everett looked at her, surprised.

"Just kidding," she laughed. "If you are."

"I'm sorry. I really should have thought about that. I'm so used to it being legal, I forget other states don't have it yet."

"You'll never get arrested for it in Austin. Us being Willie Nelson folk around here and all. But it's still a pain in the ass to get."

"Next time," he said.

"Next time," she repeated with a smile. "Zilker Park is just a few minutes from here, and it's beautiful. Lots of grass and you can see downtown. Search, *Things to do near Zilker Park.*"

"Thanks so much for—"

"I've got it. You can just leave it there." Klair smiled, and this time, it felt authentic. "Thanks for cooking."

"Any time."

Maybe he'd struck out at getting to know her, but at least Everett was leaving on a positive note.

Chapter Thirteen

EVERETT RETURNED to the guest house, gave his boot and hats another dirty look, then grabbed his fob and phone before hitting the road.

Tempted as he was to ignore Klair's advice, he really didn't want to push too hard with Evan. And while he didn't care about Zilker Park, getting to know Austin a bit better would give him something to talk to everyone about tonight. *I see why you love this place, but let me tell you about Las Orillas …*

So he went to Zilker Park, but there was nothing for him to do without a dog or a frisbee or a friend. It was a clean park with plenty of space, a large rock formation and a scattering of trees. The downtown skyline was impressive when seen from all that sprawling grass. But still it did little for Everett; he just wasn't much of a park guy. He walked around for a quarter hour or so, which only drove home how out of shape he'd allowed himself to get.

Maybe he could be a park guy, if he had a beautiful wife to picnic with. Someone like Klair, who would enjoy the spread he'd lovingly prepare for her.

Everett googled for something else to do, but none of the *18 Crazy Amazing Things to do in Austin* sounded either crazy or amazing. Barton Springs was the closest adventure: a natural pool that was sixty-eight degrees year round. Too bad he didn't have trunks, a towel, or a change of clothes.

Climbing Mount Bonnell sounded like an awful lot of work, just to look at other people's lakefront houses from up high. There were museums and gardens — from sculpture to botanical — paddle boarding and boating on Lake Travis, plus all the shopping and eating on South Congress, or anywhere else in the city.

But Everett could only pretend to be interested in museums and gardens if he had a companion. Paddle boarding and boating both meant plunking down money for the rental equipment. Shopping was out, obviously. And as for eating, he'd rather wait for whatever Evan would be cooking tonight. He could hardly wait to experience his twin's culinary gifts firsthand.

He finally decided to see a movie at the Alamo Drafthouse. Going alone was less objectionable than most of the other activities, and he could also order snacks, which would cost less than a whole meal and still save room for dinner. Unfortunately, the first showing wasn't until after noon, and that was for something in French. No thank you.

He settled for a Best of Austin Tour, promising fun and adventure while eliminating the stress of navigating the city.

But the tour turned out to be even worse than a French film. The guide had a man bun and seriously thought he was funny. And the only other guy on the tour wouldn't shut up.

Where are you from?

Are you visiting family in Austin?

What else are you planning to do while you're here?

Three hours later, Everett made it to the theater, where he ordered popcorn and a milkshake. At least the Alamo used real butter, and his shake had a shot of bourbon in it, which he told himself he deserved after such an unnecessarily frustrating morning. The film itself felt long, at least in part because Everett had a hard time paying attention. He kept thinking about Evan, his only reason for being in Austin. He could have seen this dumb disaster flick anywhere.

When he got out at a quarter to four, he thought again about stopping by the restaurant. Evan's lunch rush would be long over, with dinner still a bit away.

Now that he finally had a worthy destination, Everett enjoyed the drive.

He had imagined Texas as dry and empty, or filled with big buildings and sprawling parking lots. But Austin was thick with trees. And the traffic wasn't bad at all, at least not now. He flew down Capital of Texas Highway in his rented Mustang, racing along a straight cut of road sheared through limestone on either side. His GPS announced that Señor Sushi was ahead on the left just as he caught sight of the restaurant's sign across the street.

He waited for the light, made a U-turn, and rehearsed what he was going to say. He swallowed, the doubt creeping in.

Evan wouldn't want him to be there. Klair had told him as much.

But he was already here, and he wouldn't stay long. So Everett killed his engine and opened the door.

A man with a long white beard and a tie-dyed T-shirt that was much too large for him stopped Everett halfway to the door.

"You're not from around here." It wasn't a question.

"No … my brother is."

"You looking for something to do?" The man in tie-dye squinted at him.

What the hell? Was this some kind of scam?

"I'm just going in there." Everett pointed at the restaurant. "To see my brother."

"Why you want to eat there? You ever hear of Ginny's Little Longhorn Saloon?"

"No. Sorry." Maybe this guy was being paid to drum up business — the conversational version of a sign-spinner. He tried to step past the man.

But Tie-Dye dodged forward and stood in Everett's way. "They have Chicken Shit Bingo at Ginny's."

Now the man had Everett's attention. "What?"

"Chicken Shit Bingo," Tie-Dye repeated with no elaboration.

"People play Bingo with chicken shit?" This must be what the locals meant about keeping Austin weird.

"Folks bet on which square the chickens are gonna shit on next." Tie-Dye nodded. "And there's honky-tonk."

"Okay … well, I'll look it up. Thanks for the recommendation." Everett tried to pass the man again.

But Tie-Dye wasn't done with him. "You been to the Cathedral of Junk yet?"

The way he said *yet* made it sound like going to the Cathedral of Junk was an inevitability. "No … not yet."

"You can't actually see the cathedral from Hannemann's, but once you're in, it'll all make sense."

"Okay?"

"You'll need to call ahead before you go."

"Do you work for these places?" Everett asked.

"I work for Abraham."

"Is that another word for God?"

"No." Tie-Dye shook his head, suddenly looking at

Everett like he was stupid. "Abraham Shyer. He owns the metal shop over off Ed Bluestein."

"Okay." Everett had no idea who Ed Bluestein might be, or what else he could possibly say.

"Welcome to Austin." Tie-Dye nodded, then tipped his chin and hurried off through the parking lot, as though Everett had been the one slowing *him* down.

Everett went inside and was instantly bowled over. Pics on the website didn't do the place justice. Open layout, with a glass wall on the far end that looked out onto a handsome cactus garden. Tidy tables for two circled the perimeter, with larger round tables strategically positioned throughout the oversized room, the lot of them messily centered around what looked like a Japanese Maple reaching for the skylight above.

"Can I ... I'm sorry ... I ..." The woman seemed lost for words. She tucked a strand of hair behind her ear and tried again. "Do I know you?"

Everett touched his face, realizing that she'd noticed his resemblance to her boss.

But she had no idea who he was, which meant that even though Evan had met his twin, he didn't see that as a momentous enough occasion to share with his coworkers.

But, these were employees more than coworkers, so sharing intimate details of the boss's life probably wasn't appropriate. It wasn't like he ever told Lena where he was going.

"I'm Evan's twin brother."

"I'm Anika." She thrust out her hand like she had no idea what else to do. "I didn't know he had a brother ... especially a twin. It's nice to meet you."

"You too." Everett shook her hand. "So ... is he here?"

"Is it an emergency?"

"No ... I just ... can you please show me to the kitchen?"

"No way." An emphatic shake of her head. "I love working here."

"What does that have to do with anything?"

"No one bothers Evan when he's working. That's the rule."

"Not even his twin brother?"

"Not if you're unexpected. *Are you expected?*"

"Can you just tell him I'm here? No hurry, whenever you're back there next. I'm definitely not looking to bother him." When Anika didn't reply, he added, "Or I can just head over to his house and let him know I dropped by later."

"I'll tell him," Anika said with an uncertain smile.

Everett took a seat at the bar, working to curb his disappointment.

Ten minutes turned into twenty and Everett was really starting to doubt himself. Maybe he should have listened to Klair. He felt bad saying *nothing* when the bartender asked him what he wanted to drink, so he ordered a whiskey neat and declined a menu. If Evan didn't tell the bartender to comp his drink, he'd have to take another cash advance on his credit card.

Even slowly sipped, his drink was soon gone and Everett was seriously considering ditching Señor's. But then Evan came out from the kitchen, approaching Everett and removing his apron on the way. "I'm sorry. It's been a very busy day."

"I get it." Everett stood, pushing the empty glass away from him, hoping his brother would notice. Even if he didn't get the drink comped, it would be nice to get credit for ordering it. "Remember, I'm a restaurateur, too?"

"Right," Evan said.

Everett nodded toward the kitchen. "Anything I can do to help?"

"No, thanks. But by all means, have a meal on me."

"Oh, that's okay. Aren't we—"

"Anika!" Evan reached out and grabbed her arm as she passed. His gesture managed to appear both aggressive and gentle.

She looked from her boss to his brother. "Yeah?"

"Whatever he wants to order is on the house, okay?"

"Got it." Anika nodded, then tipped her chin toward the bar. "Drinks, too?"

"Sure." Then back to Everett. "We'll catch up later, okay?"

It wasn't a question, because Evan didn't wait for an answer.

"I'll get you a molé roll while you look over the rest of the menu," Anika told him. "Go ahead and sit wherever you want."

"Thanks," Everett mumbled.

He found a seat and looked through the menu. But he was anticipating a dinner that he'd been hoping for all day. He didn't want to fill up now.

Though he had no idea what time dinner would be, and at this point hadn't actually even been invited. Maybe he should head to the house. Harmony and Jazz would probably be home and—

No. That was the opposite of what he would do.

Everett should prove he didn't need them. Let them come to him.

The molé rolls turned out to be one of the most amazing things he had ever put in his mouth. Once done, he left his last five-dollar bill as a tip for Sierra, who'd braved Evan's wrath on his behalf.

Now it was time to get lost in Austin.

Chapter Fourteen

AND GET LOST HE DID.

Literally, for more than an hour. His GPS stopped working. Streets seemed to change names for no apparent reason, and roads that should have gone straight through from A to B ended up splitting off and branching into nowhere. Some roads had the feel of horse trails filled in with concrete.

He eventually found his way back, proud of himself for finding the Capital of Texas Highway despite his ailing navigation. From there, it was easy enough to find Bee Cave, then drive the remainder of his way to Evan's with confidence.

But it was after seven before he pulled up to the house. And despite having driven all around the city, he still didn't have a decent story to tell. Should he bitch about the tour-goer who wouldn't stop talking? Or brag about all of the nothing he spent his day on? Maybe regale his brand new family with tales of the same movie that was playing everywhere in America?

He'd never felt more like a loser.

Only after the engine was off did Everett finally realize that he had a story to tell. He'd been accosted outside of Señor Sushi by a commanding officer in the Army of Weird. Surely, that surreal conversation would be good to earn a few laughs.

He rehearsed the story in his head on his way to the front door, feeling more nervous than he should, considering he was about to see his new family. He wasn't ready to go inside, especially knowing he had to knock on the door like a stranger.

He swallowed, clenched and unclenched his fists, then turned around and walked to the gate. Better to freshen up first.

He took a fast shower, then quickly dressed in the same jeans, this time with a solid black tee. It seemed nicest for dinner, since his cowboy shirt was the only thing he had with a collar. He wished he had a better selection to choose from.

He left the guest house and stood in front of the back door, paralyzed again. Nobody told him that he wasn't welcome for dinner, but he hadn't been invited. And Evan hadn't exactly been happy to see him today.

He had a fully stocked fridge. Maybe he should just make himself something to eat, then come back after the kids were in bed.

He took out his phone and checked his messages. Nothing new, but he'd been ignoring the Ds for three days now. They'd probably given up on saving him from himself and were waiting for him to come home and cry about his inevitable failure. They loved him, but they didn't believe in him.

So he texted: *OMG, so many awesome things happening here! You guys are the best for being worried, but this might be the best deci-*

sion I've ever made. I have a twin brother! Just like you two! I can't wait to tell you more as soon as I get back!

Then he forced himself to send Clara a quick note:

Sorry I'm not in town! Great things happening. Can't wait to catch you up on the terrific news when I'm back.

Then he put his phone on silent and slipped it back in his pocket before she could reply.

He just needed a few hours of alone time with Evan, to rekindle that connection he'd felt when Evan had introduced him to his favorite whiskey. But someone had to answer the door first. He hated feeling like an unwelcome idiot.

Stop being a coward and knock on the door. NOW, Everett.

He drew a deep breath and finally knocked.

Even five seconds would have felt like forever, but it took twice that long before the back door opened and Everett found himself surprised to see a smiling Klair.

"Hey there, stranger. Perfect timing. We're just about to eat."

"Oh great ... I wasn't sure."

Another smile, then she opened the door all the way.

Everett entered, then followed her past the kitchen and into a well-appointed dining room. Looking at the same room last night, he had thought it was only for show, figuring that Evan's family must eat around the counter on the elegant bar stools, or nosh in front of the TV like a normal family. But the dining room table was set, including a place for him in between Harmony and Jazz, both of them already sitting.

Probably because they saw Everett as company, rather than family. Or maybe because they felt bad that he hadn't really had a birthday celebration of his own. Maybe this was their way of officially welcoming him into the family, now that they'd gotten used to the idea of Evan having a twin.

Everett was doubly glad that he'd taken the opportunity to cook for Klair this morning.

Jazz pointed to Everett's plate. "I think you're here."

Harmony looked at her brother. "You *think*, or you *know*?"

"Don't start," Klair said, casting a warning glance at her daughter.

"I'm not starting anything."

"Where's Evan?" Everett asked.

"I'm right here." Evan entered the dining room and took his seat at the head of the table.

"That's a bigger deal than you might realize." Klair was speaking to Everett, but looking at her husband. "Evan is constantly working these days, so we don't get family dinner nearly as often as we like. That's why we're grateful that you're eating with us tonight, Rhett. It gives this guy a reason to break bread with his family."

Everett could have done without the nickname, but the rest made him happy. "Glad to be here."

"What is this?" Jazz asked, looking down at his plate.

"It's a ready-made casserole from Central Market. I had more to deal with than expected today, so this was the best I could do."

"It's great, honey," Evan said. "Thank you."

"How often do you cook … at home, I mean?" Everett asked his brother.

"Ha!" Harmony snorted.

"Less than I'd like to." Evan grabbed his glass of water and started to drink.

"Less than we'd all like him to," Klair added.

"Mom's a great cook," Jazz said.

Harmony looked down at her ready-made casserole. "And a really terrific shopper."

"I already warned you about your mouth."

"What?" Harmony shrugged, looking at her mother with *Go ahead, I dare you* in her eyes. "I was giving you a compliment."

"It didn't sound like one." Her brother, stating the obvious.

"What's in this ready-made wonder dish?" Harmony asked.

"It's baked ziti with sausages and peppers."

"Oh, is that what's under all this cheese?"

"Jesus, Harmony." Klair shook her head and turned toward Everett. "So, Rhett, how was your day? Any adventures in Austin?"

"It was great!" But Everett didn't know where to go after that.

Jazz tried to save him. "What did you do?"

"Some touristy stuff, probably no big deal to you guys." Everett grinned. "But I did see someone who was definitely trying to keep Austin weird."

"What was he doing?" Jazz asked.

"All kinds of nonsense. He asked if I was from around here, like he could tell I wasn't an Austinite just by looking at me. Anyway, he asked if I'd ever heard of Ginny's Little Longhorn Saloon ..." The table traded glances at the mention of Ginny's saloon. "What? You guys know the place?"

"We know the place," Evan said.

"So you know about their bingo?"

"We know about their bingo," Klair confirmed.

"Oh ..." The wind was only slightly out of his sails. "So yeah, he was telling me all about their chicken ...

bingo ... but that wasn't even the weird part. He asked me if I'd ever been to a place called the—"

"Cathedral of Junk?" Evan finished his sentence.

"Yeah," Everett said, deflated.

"That's Johan Shyer," Harmony explained. "He'd be locked up if it wasn't for his brother. He really likes Dad's restaurant. Sometimes he hangs out in front of the place for hours."

"Dad hates him," Jazz said.

"I don't hate him." Evan took another drink.

"You went to Señor?" Klair seemed surprised, even though she was the one who had told Everett her husband would be there all day long in the first place.

Evan set down his glass. "So the most exciting thing that happened to you today was a minute-long conversation with a kook in front of my restaurant?"

"It just ... made me laugh." Then his eyes fell to the ready-made casserole and he started fishing through the cheese and ziti for sausage and peppers.

The conversation veered sharply away from him after that. And when they did include him, they set his teeth on edge with that damned nickname.

Did you hear that, Rhett?

I bet they don't have brisket like that in California ... eh, Rhett?

Did you catch last week's game, Rhett?

Like he should have an opinion about Texas high school football. Or bluebonnets. Or the latest addition to the Whataburger menu.

By the time everyone had polished off their casserole, Everett finally saw a way to maybe insert himself into the conversation. Evan and Klair were starting to go at it. The right advice might ingratiate him to them both.

"I'm not asking you to take a week off of work ..." Klair kept pressing. Their exchange was only a minute old, but by the sigh in Evan's eyes and voice, it might as well have been ancient. "I'm asking for one night."

"It's not just any night," Evan argued. "It's a week before the restaurant opens."

"If we do it any later, then it will be a week after you open and you'll be barking about how much you're needed more than ever."

"Or—"

"*Or*," Klair kept going, ignoring Evan's interruption, "it'll be a month later after Tequila Mockingbird takes off and you'll be telling me that you've never felt so short-staffed. So, when exactly—"

"Do we really have to do this now?" Evan asked with a glance toward his brother.

"No, of course not," Klair said with a scary little smile. "When would you like to pencil it in? According to my calendar it can't be at any time before the restaurant opens, or at any time after, so … is *never* best for you?"

Everett couldn't tell if Harmony and Jazz were squirming in their seats because they were embarrassed that 'Uncle Rhett' was seeing their parents fight, or if they were upset by the argument itself.

Everett suggested the obvious solution. "If all you really want is a date night, why don't you eat at Señor Sushi? You guys could still have a night out together, while Evan would be available if things got out of hand at the restaurant?"

Evan looked at Everett like he was an idiot, and Klair appeared to be grinding her teeth.

Harmony broke the silence. "Way to go, Rhett."

Another several moments of awkward quiet, then Jazz asked if they were having dessert.

"We have carrot cake," Klair said.

Harmony licked her lips. "Mmmm … Central Market-licious."

Klair stood without responding to her daughter and stomped to the kitchen. No one spoke while she was gone, and her return felt like a mercy killing when she came marching back to the table with six separate slices of cake, carrying them like a waitress — one extra just in case someone wanted seconds, or to keep her load symmetrical.

"Thanks for the help, Harmony," Klair said as she delivered plates of freshly sliced carrot cake across the table.

"Jazz could have helped."

"You call me a suck-up whenever I offer!"

Everett picked at his slice of cake as they ate in silence. It was obvious that no one wanted him around. He should have kept his mouth shut, then lent Evan a sympathetic ear while Klair did the dishes.

To Everett's surprise, Klair suggested that they all move outside to the pool.

"I have homework," Harmony said.

"Fine, go upstairs and do your homework, then," Klair replied, sounding too tired for what was clearly a very regular argument.

Harmony disappeared, then the remaining four of them shuffled outside.

Klair lit some candles — "or the mosquitos will kill us," she said — while Jazz sat in a lawn chair off to the side and started scrolling on his phone. Evan took a seat in front of a darkened fire pit, and Everett sat beside him.

"Thank you for all of this. I really appreciate you taking me in."

"Nothing to it," Evan said with an anemic smile. "It's just a couple of days."

"A couple of days with my twin brother?" Everett kept

his voice bright. "That's a couple more days than I ever expected to have."

Evan didn't reply, so Everett asked, "What was it like when you first found out that you were adopted?"

"It wasn't really like that." Evan shrugged. "My sister and I always knew."

"Oh ... that's right ... I forgot about your sister." Everett waited for Evan to follow up his answer with something else, like maybe a question about Everett's experience. But none came. "What about at school — did anyone ever make fun of you for being adopted?"

"Not really." Evan shook his head. "I mean, sure, kids are kids, but nothing serious."

"Oh." *Good for you.*

More silence.

Everett needed a different route to reach his destination.

Klair had vanished back inside after lighting the candles, as if getting them all out of the house was only a ploy to give her enough space to hide from the company she couldn't ask to leave. Jazz didn't appear to be paying attention to their conversation with his nose just inches away from his phone.

Everett lowered his voice. A risky move, but here he went anyway. "Is there any way you could maybe take a day off before the new restaurant opens? For Klair, I mean. Not that it's my place to say anything, but that sure seems like it would really mean a lot to her."

Evan looked over at his brother, clearly irritated. "I love Klair, but she has no idea how hard the restaurant business actually is."

"I think she understands. She just misses you."

"Okay." Evan obviously had zero interest in having a

genuine conversation with his brother, and Everett had butted in enough for one night.

Time to find some common ground with his twin.

"Oh … Did you always want to be a chef?"

"I graduated from college with a degree in business management, then got my MBA and went to culinary school."

"Then you opened your restaurant?" Culinary school had been Everett's dream, but his grades were never good enough for a scholarship.

"I apprenticed in a four-star restaurant before opening Señor."

"What's next, after Tequila Mockingbird?"

Evan gave him a heavy sigh. "We have an investor talking about franchising, but I'm not sure that's the kind of leap I want to make. At least not yet."

"Oh yeah, why?"

"Because I want everything with my name on it to maintain a certain level of quality, and two restaurants will be hard enough to manage for a while. I'd rather focus on building my reputation as a world-class chef."

"Makes sense. My cafe is doing well, if you're ever looking to share recipes or, you know, do a bit of cross-pollination."

"Thanks," Evan said.

Jazz looked up. "Is it okay if go inside?"

"Of course." Evan smiled at his son, and Everett couldn't help but think that he wanted to go with him.

But at least they were finally alone.

"What about you? What was it like when you found out that you were adopted?" Evan finally asked.

"My parents didn't tell me until I was ten, but I knew a long time before that." Everett decided it was time to get real. "My brothers hated me. They were a lot older, and never wanted me around. They told me first chance they got, and they never let me forget it. At first, I didn't believe them, but as I got older I saw how different we looked. They said that they'd kill me if I told Mom or Dad that I knew, and I believed them."

"I'm sorry to hear that," Evan said, and it sounded like he truly meant it.

"My brothers were always beating me up," Everett continued. "My dad knew, but he didn't care. Mom couldn't have any more children after my brother Marco was born. She wanted another kid, but Dad obviously didn't. At least not one from outside his gene pool."

"That sucks."

Everett found himself smiling. "I was always so jealous of the connection my older brothers had with each other. The way they could finish one another's sentences or communicate with a look. They each always seemed to know what the other one was thinking. And they always backed each other up, no matter what."

"So you guys had nothing in common?"

"*Nothing.* They played varsity football in high school and dated cheerleaders. They were both prom kings in their respective senior years. And class presidents. Not because they cared about school politics. They were just great at being popular. It was the opposite for me. I never made the cut, even though I tried out for the football team all four years, and I never went to prom because I didn't want to go alone."

"But you had friends, right?"

"Oh yeah, my best friends, the Ds. Devon and Derek. They're twins."

"I remember you mentioning them."

"It was weird, growing up with twins for best friends."

"In what way?" Evan asked.

"They were always there for me, but ..." It was hard to admit this next bit, so Everett sort of just spit it out. "I was just always so jealous of them, too."

"I guess that makes sense."

His throat tightened, and he took a big gulp of whiskey while he braced himself for the next admission. It was the thing he wanted to share most with his brother — but he didn't want to cry in front of him, not when they still barely knew each other.

"My mom died a couple of weeks ago. She was the only one in the family who cared about me, and all the good stuff about me ... it came from her. My happiest times as a little kid were when I would follow her around the kitchen, learning her recipes."

Evan smiled. "That sounds familiar."

"I'm a great cook, and an even better baker ... I just wish I was better at the business side of things."

"It takes a lot of practice."

"And an MBA," Everett laughed.

"Yeah, that helps."

Another silent moment, but this one felt nice.

"Anyway," Everett started the conversation again. "My adoption was sealed, but I kept getting more and more curious about where I came from, so I eventually hired a private eye to track down my birth parents. That's what led me here to you. Man, you should have seen me the day I found out that I had a twin brother."

He turned to Evan, wanting to see his face for this next part.

"I know I dropped in out of nowhere, but what did you think ... when you opened the door and saw that you had a twin?"

It took too long before Evan answered. Enough for Everett's heart to start beating faster.

Evan set a comforting hand on his brother's shoulder. "I always knew I had a twin."

"What?"

Everett had never felt more destroyed. He'd rather be suffering yet another beating from his adopted brothers than facing the truth that his biological brother had known about him, and not cared.

"Why didn't you ever come looking for me?" Then, because that barely scratched at the bigger question. "You obviously had the resources."

Evan squeezed his shoulder before letting it go. "I wished you well, brother, but I was happy with the family I had."

"Oh." Another word and Everett would start crying for sure.

Evan seemed to sense it. "Even though I never reached out, I'm glad you drove to Austin and that I'm getting to know you now."

Everett smiled and buried his aching as best he could.

But it was too little, too late.

Chapter Fifteen

Everett groaned as he checked his phone — almost nine.

So much for getting up early enough to catch Evan before work. He must have turned the alarm off in his sleep. But maybe that was better? His stomach still ached from the gut-punch of Evan's admission last night. How could he know about Everett but not care enough to reach out?

Worse, Everett wasn't sure if he'd have done the same in Evan's position. If he'd had everything a child could want, would he have cared that Evan might be suffering halfway across the country?

Probably not. And admitting that made Everett feel wrong for coming here and intruding on his brother's perfect life.

Well, almost perfect. Apparently Klair wasn't entirely happy with Evan. Did it make Everett a bad person to feel relieved that he wasn't the only one struggling to balance a career and a significant other?

Speaking of which, it was time to return Clara's call, now that he could finally report some success. He couldn't claim an instant soul-bond with his newfound twin, but he could say that they'd celebrated their shared birthday without lying.

"Oh, amazing," she said when she picked up. "You finally learned how to use your phone. Did you need to take an online course for that, or were you able to find a simple how-to article?"

"Is everything okay?" Everett felt a sudden and perhaps unreasonable fear that *no*, things were absolutely not in any way okay. Something awful had happened with Jimi while he was fifteen hundred miles away and unable to help.

"Everything is fine, assuming you can do your job as Jimi's other parent."

"What's that supposed to mean?"

"I got an audition."

"Oh yeah? That's great."

"For lead guitarist in A Splinter of Moon."

"Wow. Prodigious!" How had she managed that? A Splinter of Moon was Clara's favorite band, and one of the biggest influences on what she referred to as "her personal sound."

Clara sighed, clearly annoyed that he hadn't responded with more enthusiasm. "So I need you to take Jimi, for at least the next three days. I can drop him off at your place in an hour."

"I can't, Clara. I'm in Texas."

"TEXAS?"

"Austin. My brother is here. I came to visit."

"I saw Marco and Roberto at the grocery store last night."

"I hired a private eye to find my birthparents. Turns out I had a twin brother living in Austin."

"I'm guessing that this is the 'really great news' you were going to tell me about later?"

"You wouldn't believe how many similarities there are between us. It's like all those stories you hear about identical twins. He's married to a Klair instead of a Clara—"

"We're not married."

"— and she's a musician, too. Her band is called Redheaded Stepchild — have you ever heard of them? They're opening for the Stray Bullets. Anyway, my brother, Evan, owns two restaurants here in Austin. I know I only have the one, and both of his are a little bigger than mine, but—"

"That wouldn't be hard." Clara paused. "Are you guys really identical?"

"He's my spitting image." Except for being in much better shape, with a much better haircut, and a much better life.

"Is he allergic to exercise, too?"

"You don't have to be mean."

"When are you coming home?"

"I'm not sure."

A long silence, then, "Fuck you, Everett."

"I've asked you to please not swear at me like that."

"Well, I asked you to start being a goddamned grown-up and look where we are."

"I know it's not your first choice, but you *can* take Jimi to your mom's."

"Not for three days. No way."

"Why do you need three days for an audition?"

"Because it's in Nashville!"

"How was I supposed to know that?"

"By doing the math, Everett. Goddammit, I knew you'd fuck this up for me!"

"I'm sorry your audition is in Nashville. If I'd known, I could have delayed my trip. I just wanted to be here for my twin brother's birthday party. By the way, thanks for wishing me a happy—"

"Oh, fuck you and your birthday week! We're not married anymore. I don't have to treat you like a goddamned ten-year-old."

"That's not fair," Everett said.

"You know what's not fair? You taking off to Texas without telling me."

"I have a twin brother now. Why can't you understand how important family is to me?"

There was a long silence.

"You need to get current on your child support," Clara finally said.

"*What?*"

"You heard me. I've been cutting you slack because the cafe hasn't been doing well, but if you can afford an impromptu trip to Texas, you can afford to support your son. Who is *also* a member of your family."

"You've gotta be kidding me!"

"About what, Everett? That you owe me thousands of dollars in child support? Or do you not believe that Jimi is your son?"

"All I'm asking is for you to think about what I'm going through for once."

Now Clara was yelling. "You're *always* 'going through' something."

"That's not true and you know it."

"Are you going to come back here and take responsibility for your son?"

"I just need—"

"It's a yes or no question, Everett."

"The Ds would watch him for a few days—"

"You can't dump Jimi on your friends. It's not fair to your son, and incidentally, it's also not fair to your friends who have families of their own to take care of."

"Even if I could get back there in time—"

Clara hung up.

Chapter Sixteen

You're always going through something.

The only way to get Clara's words out of Everett's head was for him to prove her wrong.

If he wanted to connect with his brother, then he needed to make a deliberate effort, instead of waiting around for Evan to hand him an engraved invitation.

After a rushed shower and a quick check of his dwindling bank account, Everett headed for the main house. He straightened his shoulders in front of the back door, ready to knock, and confident enough to do so without acting like a baby this time.

Or a ten-year-old.

He raised his knuckles, but they never made it to the glass.

He could hear a noise inside. Low voices.

Maybe he should have knocked, or turned right around and gone back to the guest house. But Everett couldn't do either. Something compelled him to put his hand on the doorknob, then that same something insisted he turn it.

He closed the door softly behind him, surprised to

realize that one of the voices was Evan's. He wasn't at work after all. He was in the kitchen, arguing with Klair.

Everett stopped walking and peeked around the corner.

At a glance, it looked like Evan was having a meltdown and Klair was trying to calm him.

"So you're really going to look me in the eye and tell me that this isn't total fucking bullshit?" He stared at Klair, apparently waiting for her to answer what sounded like a rhetorical question.

"No," she said calmly. "It's clearly bullshit. I'm trying to say that it's not the end of the world."

He ran a hand across his stubbled face. "Well, it's the end of *our* world."

"Our world isn't the new restaurant, Evan."

"That's not what I'm saying."

"Then what are you saying?"

"THAT THIS IS A TOTAL FUCKING DISASTER!"

Everett shouldn't be standing here. He needed to turn around and return to the guest house, come back and try again later. But just as he was about to take a long and quiet step backward, Klair made a half-turn and caught his gaze.

To his tremendous surprise, she gave him a smile, then turned back to her husband without alerting him to Everett's presence.

"I just lost one of the two station chefs for Tequila. He's going to be in the hospital for a month." Evan shook his head. "What the hell was he doing skiing two weeks before our big opening?"

"You promised him a long weekend after a murderous few months. To bond with his family before things got stupid crazy again."

"BUT SKIING? He couldn't have picked something less likely to fuck him up — like swimming with sharks?"

"Who do you think is more upset about their broken leg, Evan? You or Gabriel?"

"Seriously? Me."

"Gabriel has three children. How do you think they're feeling right now? What about his wife?"

"I'm not saying that they don't matter, Klair. But their misery doesn't solve our problem."

"Why don't you use one of Señor's station chiefs until Gabriel is back?"

"You really think I haven't already considered that?" Evan shook his head again, looking disappointed in her. "We're already understaffed, with our current station chefs working six days a week. I'd have to close the first restaurant until I could hire someone else."

"You're always so dramatic."

And this was sounding so familiar.

"Why not ask Angelo if he has any extra help? Or Blythe?"

"I'm not solving this problem by poaching staff."

"It's not poaching if the person is extra."

"Who has anyone *extra?*" Evan threw his hands in the air.

"I don't know," Klair said, "maybe restaurants that aren't that busy."

"Sorry. I don't have any friends with shit restaurants."

"It would never hurt to ask."

"No way." Evan shook his head, almost violently.

"Why are you so stubborn?"

"I'm not being stubborn, or even 'rigid' like you always accuse me of being. But I know how I would feel if one of my friends asked if I had 'anyone I could spare.' I'd think it was bullshit, then do what I could to help them."

"See, you would want to help them."

"Did you miss the part about how I would also be pissed?"

"So all chefs are assholes?"

"No less than you rockstars."

"I'm hardly a rockstar," Klair said.

"But Lord, aren't you trying?" Evan drew a deep breath and opened his mouth. But then he turned ever so slightly and saw his brother. "Everett … how long have you been there?"

Everett stepped forward. "I'm sorry to hear about your station chef."

"So, a while," Evan said.

"A couple of minutes," Klair corrected him.

"Why didn't you say anything?"

"What did you want me to say, Evan? You would have been pissed if I interrupted you mid-rant, and equally pissed if I didn't. Because right now, you're pissed about everything. Besides, it's not like we were discussing where we buried our stolen diamonds."

"I'm sorry you had to see that," Evan said to Everett.

"That was nothing. You should have heard the call I just had with my ex-wife." Should he have admitted that? "So, how will not having the station chef affect things?"

"It's a total disaster," Evan said.

"I get that … but our restaurants are different." Everett laughed, sounding uncomfortably self-conscious. "I don't have a station chef. What does losing yours mean for the restaurant?"

"We'll have to delay the opening for sure."

"Is that a bad thing? I mean, is it possible that delaying the opening by a few weeks will end up being one of those things that ultimately proves the adage, 'everything happens for a reason'?"

"He really hates that saying," Klair said.

"Not a goddamn chance." Evan shook his head.

"Why?" Everett asked. "Is there a bunch of press lined up or something?"

"Or *something*." Evan sighed. "If we delay the opening, all the money we've spent on promotion goes to waste. *Tribeza* magazine was going to do a feature on us, but who knows how many months they book those in advance. We have people flying in who won't reschedule. And if we flop on opening night, it could take us a year or more to recover our reputation."

"And those opportunities weren't all paid for with money," added Klair. "Evan's dad managed to land a lot of great publicity for us by pulling some strings and calling in favors."

Everett lit up with the answer. "What about a temp agency? Your station chef doesn't need to be amazing so much as competent, right?"

"Are you kidding?" Klair laughed. "Competent doesn't even begin to cut it for Evan."

Apparently Evan agreed. "I'm going to have to close Señor Sushi until Gabriel's back on his feet, so that both Morris and Bernardo can come to the new place. Which means we lose a month of revenue that we need to pay the loans for the remodel on the new place. And if Tequila flops, we might not be able to catch up on those payments before our loan goes into default."

"What if you only closed each restaurant for part of the day? Open Señor Sushi for lunch, and Tequila Mockingbird for dinner?"

"We've got a lot of important people coming in, but we can't control when they'll arrive," Evan said. "Tequila has to be open for both meals. Dammit, Gabriel!"

How important could any one customer be? Were they

hoping that B-list movie star was going to come in and bless the new restaurant with a Livelyfe post?

"Wow. Is there anything I can do to help?" He wanted Evan to ask him so badly, Everett could hardly breathe. This was his chance. The reason he'd felt compelled to come to Austin. So that he could cook side-by-side with his brother. And after pulling through this crisis together, their bond would be as undeniable as it would be unbreakable.

"Thanks, man, I just don't think there's anything you can do."

What? Evan's entire business was about to collapse for the lack of a station chef, but Everett wasn't good enough to sub in for a few weeks?

"I'm not saying I'm good enough to take anyone's place, but I do know how to cook, and from what I've heard, I'm not half bad." Everett let out a light, self-depre-cating laugh before he continued. "You will have to train *someone*, right?"

"Yes, I'll have to train someone, but—"

"But nothing," Klair said, cutting him off. "You've already ruled out all the other options, and you're not just risking Tequila Mockingbird by saying no, you're risking Señor Sushi too. You could bankrupt us."

"I'm processing. Is that not okay?"

She turned to Everett. "Are you really willing to derail your life for a month to help us?"

"Isn't that what family is for?"

Evan was breathing heavily through his nose, looking from Klair to Everett and back again, looking ready to detonate.

Klair glared at him, her expression full of *don't you dare*.

"I just want to help. I'll do anything," Everett tried again.

"If you really want to help, then the next time you

decide to storm a person's life unannounced, you might want to consider their schedule first."

Then Evan turned and left the kitchen without another word.

Klair looked at Everett with humiliation in her eyes. "Sorry about that."

"He didn't say *no*."

"You know it's not about you, right?" She cast her eyes to the floor, shook her head, then looked back up at Everett with a smile. "So, why were you coming inside?"

"Oh … I just wanted to say hi."

"*Hi.*" She gave him a little wave.

Then nothing.

Eventually, Everett leaned forward and whispered. "Now that we're alone …"

"Yeah?"

"Do you want to tell me where those diamonds are buried?"

Klair laughed, and the sound was more beautiful than any song by A Splinter of Moon.

Chapter Seventeen

WANTING to leave Klair on a high note, Everett bid her adios and went outside, plunking down in a pool chair to stare at the shimmering water.

He would give Evan space to calm down before they talked about what he'd be doing as his new station chef. Once they were in the kitchen together, they'd fall into a comfortable rhythm and the twin bond would finally kick in. By the time Gabriel's leg healed, they'd be so close that any future separation would be unthinkable.

Unless … Evan was so mad about being ambushed that he'd poach someone else's station chef, risking his reputation with the other local restauranteurs.

Or maybe he'd close Señor Sushi, risking both restaurants to spite his brother.

In Evan's position, would he be that petty? Everett imagined Lena quitting and Clara railroading him into hiring a replacement he didn't want, and he had to admit that yes, he would be that petty, if it meant effectively proving a stupid point: that he was willing to cut off his nose to spite his face.

But Evan was better than that. Wasn't he? Would he have one successful restaurant if he was like Everett in that way?

A sound startled him — someone on the other side of the gate, working the latch to get inside. Everett stiffened in his seat, not quite sure who it might be. A member of the family would almost for sure come through the front door, but it could be pool cleaners, landscapers, or someone making a delivery.

The side gate swung open.

And Everett saw Jazz before the boy saw him. And by the look of things, he hadn't been wrong about the family being more likely to use the front door. The kid was clearly sneaking in. His black eye and blood-crusted nose told Everett a story he already knew by heart.

"Jazz," he called out, loud enough to nab the boy's attention, but soft enough to avoid alerting Klair inside.

Jazz looked over, surprised to see Everett sitting by the pool.

"Are you okay?" Everett asked.

The boy straightened and adopted an air of bravado. "Yeah, of course. Why wouldn't I be?"

"Don't feel bad. I used to get beat up all the time." He expected Jazz to say something like, *You did?* But instead the kid just looked at him. So he added, "My brothers, usually."

Jazz hesitated, one hand still on the gate.

"Anything you want to talk about?"

"Not even a little bit."

"Okay, fair enough. Can I at least suggest that you ice your eye and your nose?"

Jazz said nothing.

"Seriously. You don't want your face to swell up any

more than it already has. It's going to hurt a lot more later."

Jazz shrugged, like he didn't care, but he took a step closer.

"I'll get some ice from the guest house."

Everett was pleased to see Jazz waiting for him in one of the pool chairs when he returned with a kitchen towel-wrapped baggie full of ice.

"Have you opened the Infinite Fidelity?"

Jazz shook his head. "I'm not allowed to yet."

"Oh yeah? Why not?"

"I need to get my report card first."

"Ah, I see …" Everett paused, hopeful.

Jazz finally asked, "Why did your brothers always beat you up?"

"Because they were assholes."

Jazz laughed.

"Seriously, it was because they were a lot older and never wanted me around."

"Harmony never wants me around."

"She's not the one who punched you, is she?"

Jazz shifted the ice bag to the other side of his face. "What's the worst thing your brothers ever did to you?"

"Once when I was really little, I think like six or seven, my parents took a vacation together. The first time they ever left me alone with them. Roberto was in charge, and he was already eighteen at the time. My parents weren't even gone for five minutes before my brothers started beating the crap out of me. When they got bored of that, they locked me in my room."

"Whoa," Jazz said. "The worst thing Harmony's ever done is steal my money."

"Your sister stole money from you?"

"Once, yeah. It was a long time ago."

"What did your parents do?"

"I never told them."

"Wow," Everett said, surprised. "Why not?"

"I think she was using it to help a friend."

"Oh. That's really understanding of you."

"Yeah. Isaiah. He's a—"

"Jazz Joshua Shepherd!" Klair exploded out of the back door and marched in an angry line right toward them.

Every muscle in Everett's body tightened. For the first time, Klair reminded him of Clara at her most furious.

"Would you like to guess who I just got off the phone with?" Klair demanded, glaring at her son.

"Mrs. Johnson?"

"That's right, Mrs. Johnson. And what do you think she said?"

"I don't know." He looked at the ground.

"I think you do. So tell me, Jazz: *What did Mrs. Johnson say?*"

He swallowed, needing another long moment. Then, "That I got into a fight."

"It looks like you walked home on your face, so I'm not sure I would have needed Mrs. Johnson to inform me of that. I'm much more interested in the details of your little scuffle. So why don't you share those with me?"

"Mrs. Johnson already told you," Jazz practically mumbled.

"Do you really want to make this any worse for yourself than it already is?" Klair was no longer yelling, but there was fire in her eyes and if Everett were Jazz he would never dare to ignore her.

"I should go—"

"Sit down, Everett," Klair said as he stood. "We're not doing him any favors by making this easier on him. If it's harder for Jazz to tell this story with you here, then *good.*"

He didn't mention that the kid was probably seconds from spilling the narrative anyway, if Klair had stayed in the house. And Everett would have heard a version that wasn't delivered under duress.

He sat, fingers still clenched around the edges of his seat.

Klair turned back to her son. "There's no band joining you onstage. This is a solo performance and the instrument is your mouth. So once again, *last time*: tell me what happened."

"I stood up for myself." He straightened his shoulders as evidence. "Just like you and Dad always taught me."

"*No, Jazz.* We taught you to stand up for yourself with words, and to set the example for who you want to be with your behavior. Not by getting into fights."

"That's what *you* taught me," Jazz said, now standing up for himself on the home front. "Dad said that sometimes you have to clench your fists and stand like a man if you want something to stop."

Klair was chewing on her bottom lip, clearly furious. "Specifically, Jazz. Don't push me. How did you stand up for yourself?"

"You remember Isaiah Ponce?"

"Of course I remember Isaiah."

"I can only take so much, Mom."

"He's been giving you a hard time since eighth grade. What's the difference now?"

"I can't take it anymore." Jazz wiped at his tears, starting to cry.

"*What* can't you take?" She softened her voice. "Please, just tell me what happened."

"Isaiah called me a tranny."

Klair sighed. "Well, are you?"

Jazz looked up at her. "Am I what?"

"A tranny?"

"No." He shook his head.

"Do you know what a tranny is?"

Jazz held her gaze. "It's someone who used to be a boy and changes themselves into a girl."

"Or a girl into a boy. So, have you had an operation that I don't know about?"

Jazz shook his head.

"Have you scheduled surgery behind my back?"

"No." Jazz stopped shaking his head, but now that tiny smile was back at the corner of his mouth.

Everett watched the scene in disbelief, wondering what life would have been like if he'd had a parent — or anyone in his family — who cared enough to ever talk to him like that.

"So," Klair continued, "why do you care so much that Isaiah Ponce called you a tranny?"

"Because … he can't just call me that."

"You're right, Jazz. He shouldn't be calling *anyone* that. Whether or not someone identifies as trans, that word is extremely offensive."

"That's what I'm trying to say!"

"No." Klair shook her head. "You weren't sticking up for trans students, Jazz. You were defending your own ego."

"He started it."

"Well, congratulations. You ended it. Now Isaiah has to get a cap at the dentist because you knocked out one of his teeth."

"He deserved it," Jazz mumbled.

"Are you really not understanding what's happening here?" Her voice was back to loud and confrontational.

"Go to your room."

"But, Mom—"

"*But nothing.*" She shook her head. "You know the rules. Fighting isn't tolerated in this family under any circumstances."

"You and Dad fight all the time."

"With words, Jazz. You want to throw down instead, then you can go upstairs and wait for your father to come home. No phone, no iPad, no games, no anything. Write your feelings in a notebook if you want to. Or you can sit on your bed and think."

"This isn't fair."

"You're right, it isn't. This is the last thing I should have to be dealing with right now."

Jazz looked over at Everett with pleading eyes, as if there was anything he could do.

"He can't save you, and neither can anyone else," Klair said. "Now go to your room."

Jazz opened his mouth and Everett expected one last Hail Mary argument, but instead his shoulders slumped and he shuffled away in defeat.

"And you better not slam that door!" Klair called as he neared it.

She waited for it to softly close, then fell into the seat beside Everett, visibly upset.

"Are you okay?"

After several seconds, she rolled her head toward him and said, "No, Everett. I'm not."

"Is there anything I can do to help?"

"This just started a few months ago," Klair replied, though it wasn't really an answer.

"I thought you said this kid has been bothering him since the eighth grade?"

"Isaiah Ponce is an asshole. But that doesn't mean it's

okay for Jazz to send anyone who hassles him to the hospital."

"You mean the dentist?"

"I mean any of it. Jazz was always the easy one. I *expect* Harmony to give us trouble, but …" Klair let her last sentence hang, but Everett didn't think she wanted him to fill the silence. "This is all happening because Evan isn't around. Jazz is trying to get his attention."

"I don't know," Everett dared. "Sometimes a bullied kid can hit his limit. Maybe this was something he needed to do."

Klair turned to look at Everett full-on. "*Something he needed to do?*"

"My brothers used to beat me up every chance they got. I was just telling Jazz a story right before you came outside. They hated me."

"They're your brothers. They couldn't really *hate you*."

"My mom's funeral was just over a week ago. That's when they told me they never wanted to see me again. *At the funeral.*"

"Oh … I'm so sorry to hear that."

"It doesn't matter. Fuck them. The point is, sometimes it's healthier to fight back. I could never hit my brothers, because they were so much bigger. But one time I saw a TV show where this guy kept getting his lunch stolen at work, so he put a chocolate bar in his lunch that was actually a laxative. That's how he found out who was stealing from him. So I saved my money and bought a bunch of chocolate laxatives, then left them on the dining room table when our parents weren't home because I knew my brothers would eat them."

"That's better than fighting."

"Is it?" Everett asked.

"Jazz knocked out a tooth!"

"My brothers got dangerously dehydrated. My mom was furious. She said that I could have done permanent damage to their digestive system."

"So you got into big trouble?"

"That's actually why I'm telling you this story." Sharing the memory felt good. "My mom would 'punish me' by making me do stuff like help her with dinner. And so those 'consequences' led to some of our best moments together."

"So she rewarded you for—"

"Not at all." He shook his head. "But she did use that disciplinary time as an opportunity to bond and help me grow up, instead of making me feel even more alone than I already was."

After a moment, Klair said, "Thank you, Everett. That's very helpful."

Everett smiled.

He had an ally now.

Chapter Eighteen

KLAIR HAD INSISTED that they take Everett out, as a belated birthday celebration. Secretly pleased, he'd protested at length that it wasn't necessary and that meeting his long-lost twin was the best gift of all. Evan argued that they were too close to the opening of Tequila to spare him for an evening, but Klair wouldn't drop it. She suggested that they take Everett's suggestion and have dinner at Señor Sushi, where Evan could keep an eye on things.

The restaurant was packed, with an hour-long wait, but of course Evan had a table reserved in the back. As Sierra led them there, Everett thought of his café and flushed with embarrassment. For Java Joe's, two small groups of customers was a rush. Lena constantly complained that she couldn't afford to eat lunch on her daily tips.

Once they were seated, Everett scanned the menu. The intro on the first page explained that Evan had been inspired by takoraisu, a deconstructed taco popular in Japan. He'd wanted to explore how Japanese cuisine could be married to the Tex-Mex flavors he'd been raised with.

The menu featured sushi made with locally caught fish, served on Texas-grown rice, ginger slices pickled with cumin and garlic, and wasabi with a tinge of lime juice and habanero paste.

To the yakisoba — pan-fried noodles with meat and veggies — Evan had added bacon, roasted garlic, and crushed chipotles.

He'd turned takoyaki into a deconstructed fajita, embedding seasoned chicken, steak, or shrimp in the traditional egg pancake, along with grilled onions, peppers and tomatoes, topping it all with melted cheddar, jack cheese, and pico de gallo.

Evan's teriyaki sauce was made with soy, brown sugar, and mild guajillo chilies, but customers who wanted it spicier could swap in a version made with jalapeños. The meat was barbecued instead of pan-fried.

Even the gyoza were Tex-Mex: the deep-fried dumplings were filled with pork al-pastor and dipped in a spicy pineapple-mango-habanero sauce.

And of course, Evan's version of takoraisu. A generous pile of brisket on cilantro-lime rice, topped with Oaxacan cheese, caramelized onions, shredded cabbage, salsa, and crema.

They also had a variety of different margaritas. Klair ordered one right away, despite Evan's obvious scowl of displeasure. But before he could start an argument, one of the other waitresses asked Evan if he'd mind handling something in the kitchen.

"Be right back," Evan said as he stood. "Shall I choose for the table while I'm there?"

"Maybe Everett would like to choose his own meal, like an adult," Klair said.

Whatever was going on between Klair and Evan,

Everett wanted to stay out of it. "Everything looks delicious, I'm up for whatever you recommend."

Evan hurried away as Sierra brought a huge margarita for Klair and a bowl of spicy edamame for the table.

Klair started in on her drink while the kids buried themselves in their phones. Thankfully Evan came back a moment later, looking annoyed.

"How often does the menu change?" Everett asked, hoping to get the conversation going.

"Whenever my husband gets bored. That's what he does whenever things start to slow down, he adds something new to his plate."

"Come on, Klair. Do we have to do this now?"

"That's exactly what I'll be thinking to myself each and every time you get up from our dinner table to deal with something else in the kitchen."

"What do you want me to do? Because I'm getting really burned out on feeling like I can't get anything right."

She swallowed the last of her habanero margarita, then held up her empty glass and called out to a passing server. "One more of these, please."

A second server approached the table and whispered in Evan's ear. The server left and he sighed. "Sorry, I have to go. I'll be right back."

"Of course you do." Klair gave her empty glass a dirty look.

"This is me doing my job."

"Really, Evan? Because I would have thought that your job is being the father in this family."

"Yes, Klair, that is one of my jobs. So is making sure this place is running smoothly instead of falling apart, so we can all keep living in Westlake and enjoying the life my hard work provides."

"Right. Because I don't contribute anything."

"That's not what I said."

"Your son got in a fight at school today. He has a black eye."

"I can see that."

"Well, noticing but not caring enough to say a word about it is worse than being oblivious."

Evan didn't respond. At least not verbally.

He pushed himself away from the table, then stood and marched off to the kitchen.

Sierra dropped off another habanero margarita for Klair, who winked and said, "Keep 'em coming. Do you want anything, Rhett?"

"No, thank you." He shook his head and the server walked away. Harmony was still glued to her screen and Jazz kept shifting in his seat while casting his gaze wildly around the restaurant. Everett turned to Klair. "How many is that now?"

"Is there a reason you're keeping count?" She glared at him.

Several painfully long minutes passed. Klair was on her way to getting wildly drunk. Thank goodness Evan was on his way back to the table.

"I'm really sorry, you guys." And he sounded it. "The food will be out in a couple more minutes. I got our dishes started."

After he sat down, Evan reached across the table, waited for Klair to finish sipping and set her glass on the table, then he put his hand on top of hers. "I know you feel like I'm ignoring you, or putting the restaurant ahead of you. I can't apologize enough for that. You have my word: once Tequila is running, I'll slow down, and prepare better for the next time. Third time's the charm."

"Why does there have to *be* a third time? Aren't two successful restaurants enough for you?"

"Is it enough for—?"

"Please don't start listing off all the chefs you have a boner for." She glared at him.

"It's not like this is news, Klair. More than two restaurants has always been part of the plan. I am acknowledging that I got in over my head, and I'm doing it in front of company."

Company?

Everett knew that they didn't have a full twin bond yet, but they were brothers. Didn't that count for anything?

"You act like I don't understand the situation." Now Klair was really slurring her words. "But I understand everything."

Evan didn't respond, probably hoping that Klair would stop talking, or at least fill her mouth with more margarita. Harmony had finally stopped looking at her phone and was slumped low in her seat. Jazz slumped even lower.

Klair turned to Everett. "Don't you think it's a shame …" Her pause was long and pregnant and painful. "… how much some people care more about their career than their family?"

This was terrible. When Marco and Roberto had excommunicated him, Everett figured that at least he was through with family situations that made him want to jump right out the nearest window.

He and Clara fought regularly, but only once or twice in front of Jimi. And not even once in front of *company*. "It's hard to balance work and family—"

"So you don't think your twin brother is shitting the bed?"

"How many of those have you had?" Evan gestured at Klair's newest margarita.

"That's exactly what *he* wanted to know!"

Evan turned to Everett. "How many of these has she had?"

"I'm not sure." *Too many.*

"Don't involve him in our little … spat," she finally finished.

"I think you've already done that." Evan shook his head. "This isn't like you."

"Maybe so you would have to drive me home."

Evan sighed. "Harmony, take your mother home. I'll grab a FASTr and get there when I can."

"But we haven't even eaten yet!" Harmony protested.

"You can't just get rid of me," Klair added, slurring even more than before. "Stop caring what everyone thinks, and start caring about what *I* think, Evan."

"I do care about what you—"

"Then why don't we ever talk anymore? Why does your brother who I barely know pay more attention to me than you do?"

"Please, Klair. Don't do this."

Everett couldn't agree more. *Please, Klair. Don't fucking do this.*

Everett's phone rang. A generic ring, so it wasn't anyone he knew. But that didn't matter at all. He would happily talk to someone about maybe changing his health insurance right now. Or about his car's extended warranty. He drew his phone like a gun from its holster and blinked down at the screen. *Unknown number.*

"So sorry." Already standing. "I have to take this."

He answered outside, just as the third ring began to trill.

"Mister Alvarez," said a voice when he answered.

"Who's this?"

"Abbot Paulson. Your landlord."

"Oh, yes. Of course. Your name didn't come up on my caller ID."

"I always get your voicemail. My odds were better calling with an unknown number."

Asshole.

"Did my rent check bounce?"

An alarmingly real possibility. If so, Everett was in much worse shape than he'd realized. The air outside had the tang of something burning. Probably the stench of his life.

"No. Your check didn't bounce. But I have news for you that I didn't want to leave on a voicemail."

"Good news?" Everett felt hopeful.

"If it were good news, I wouldn't be concerned about you insisting that you never got my message three months from now."

This wasn't good. "What happens in three months?"

"I'll be raising your rent."

Heart pounding, eyes starting to water. "How much?"

"Thirty percent," Abbot said without apology.

"You can't do that," Everett replied, on the verge of a panic attack.

"Thirty percent is the most Las Orillas will allow me to raise it."

"Why are you doing this?" Everett asked.

"It's business."

"It feels personal."

"Maybe it's a bit of both, Mister Alvarez. That corner is hot, and getting hotter. The right tenant could make a killing in your space."

"I am the right tenant. Java Joe's is going to—"

"You tell me this every time we talk. But that's all you are: *talk*. It's embarrassing how little you've done with that space."

"I have a skeleton crew."

"Mr. Alvarez, you had your chance. Now I'm giving the space to someone who'll do more with it."

"I'll get a lawyer."

"You absolutely can. But I suggest you save your money and use this a learning opportunity. The tenant who can afford the thirty percent increase, which the property is absolutely worth, will invest in renovation. You rejected my offer to match your remodeling budget. Because you didn't have one. That was my mistake, and I won't make it again."

"Is there anything I can do to change your mind?"

Abbot sighed. "If you can afford the rent increase and commit to renovations within the next year, and you can show me that you've got a plan to bring in the kind of traffic that spot can support, I'm willing to give you another shot."

"I'll figure it out before my lease is up."

"I look forward to hearing from you then. Have a good evening, Mister Alvarez."

He stumbled back into the restaurant. Made it back to the table just as Sierra placed the last dish of an elaborate spread. It looked like Evan had told the kitchen to send out half the menu.

"Is everything okay?" Evan asked.

"I'm fine," Everett said, forcing a smile.

Klair shook her finger under his nose. "No way. I've seen that face a million times. Something's wrong."

Harmony and Jazz traded a glance. They knew it too.

"I've felt the way you just looked." Evan laughed, though he sounded uncomfortable. "You sure nothing's wrong?"

"I just found out that one of my friends is having the rent raised on his business by thirty percent."

Evan winced. "Oh, that's rough."

"Derek's a good guy, but he's in way over his head," Everett lied with a shrug.

"There's no way he can pull it off?" Klair asked.

"Not a chance. Derek's the kind of guy who expects other people to solve his problems for him."

He could see it all over Evan's face: *Well, then fuck that guy.*

It was hard to disagree.

But Everett wasn't going to be like his friend "Derek."

He would solve this problem for himself, and he knew exactly how he was going to do it — by taking a page out of Evan's playbook.

Chapter Nineteen

Instead of going back to sleep when his alarm went off, Everett got up and did some stretches. Then he found a bodyweight workout on LiveLyfe that ran him through the basics — mostly push-ups, squats, lunges and crunches. He could finish the full sets, but he did each exercise until his muscles started cramping. Then he rested until he could do the next one.

It was time for him to become the Everett he could be. The one who knew who he was, because he'd finally found his twin connection.

He didn't feel the bond yet, but seeing what Evan had done with Señor Sushi inspired him. With the right attitude, and some financing from a grateful brother who would undoubtedly want to help him out once Tequila Mockingbird was a success, Everett had no doubt that he could turn Java Joe's into a trendy café that made A Hill of Beans look like slumming.

It was time to be proactive. He couldn't wait for Evan to ask him to take the station chef position. He needed to demonstrate that he was worthy to work in Evan's kitchen.

By volunteering to cook dinner for the whole family tonight.

But first, he had to convince Klair.

So, once again Everett knocked on the back door of his brother's house.

When Klair finally answered the door, she was clearly hungover. As soon as she saw him, she grunted and walked back toward the kitchen, leaving the door open for him.

He closed the door behind himself and hurried to catch up with her.

"Hey, I was thinking—"

She winced. "Not so loud."

"Sorry." He lowered his voice to a whisper. "That phone call I took last night?"

She stared at him as if he was speaking gibberish.

Right. She was probably too drunk to remember.

"Anyway, I've got to drive back to California tomorrow, to help my friend Derek out with his café. So I'd love to make dinner for the whole family tonight."

"Fine." She sat down at the kitchen table and slumped over a cup of coffee.

Great. But now for the hard part. "Do you know if Evan's planning to be home tonight?"

"He better be," she muttered. "But obviously I can't promise anything."

Everett guessed that he would, because he clearly hadn't figured out how to make peace with his wife last night, after they'd gotten home from dinner.

He felt like he should try to smooth things over, but what could he say that wouldn't make things worse?

"Please go away," Klair said. "Let me be humiliated in peace."

So he did.

· · · ·

EVERETT UNDERSTOOD NOW why Klair had said that Central Market was better than Whole Foods.

Wanting to channel his mother's spirit, he'd started at the fish counter — raised in Cabo San Lucas on the Baja Peninsula, Mom had loved seafood above all else. He was thinking of making tacos de pescado: with lightly battered and fried snapper or mahi wrapped in homemade corn tortillas, topped with crunchy cabbage, pico de gallo, and crema. And for appetizers, queso and guac.

The woman at the counter suggested that the halibut was especially great today, so he went with that. Then he loaded up with red, yellow, and orange peppers; green avocados, cilantro, and jalapeños; blue corn chips, and purple cabbage. Red tomatoes, white onions, and mango for his special pico. After some hesitation, he also bought some sweet and sour, in case Klair wanted a little hair of the margarita that had bit her last night.

The total bill was higher than Everett expected, but that's what credit cards were for, right? Life's most important moments. And this goodbye felt like one of the most important he'd ever lived.

He promised himself that he would be more mindful of his budget as soon as he got back to California.

As he unloaded the trunk back at Evan's house, the front door opened and Klair appeared on the other side, showered and looking much less hungover than before.

"Can I help you with anything?" she called.

"I just need you to hold the door for me," Everett replied, carrying a full paper bag in each arm.

He heard the door close seconds before he eased his bags onto the kitchen counter.

"Sorry about last night." She smiled. "Want some company? I could open a bottle of wine."

Everett showed her the bottle of sweet and sour. "How about a jalapeño margarita instead?"

"Ooh …" Klair made an excited face. "*Spicy.*"

"Let me get organized, then I'll start on the drinks."

"Great. See you in a few minutes," she said, then left the kitchen.

Everett didn't know if she really had something to do, or was only giving him space, but he appreciated the moment to himself either way. He emptied his bags, organizing his haul into smaller piles, before making them each a drink.

Klair returned just in time. She looked down at the drinks. "No more than two, okay? Your job is to cut me off."

"Mission accepted." Everett laughed.

Maybe he wasn't going to get to know Evan well on this trip, but he could get to know Klair better.

"So when did you know he was *the one*?" Everett asked.

"Our second date."

"Not the first or the third?" he laughed.

"The first was a disaster, and by the third, I never wanted to leave his apartment."

"When did you get married?"

"Right after he got his MBA. We wanted to wait for children, so we could each focus on our careers. Evan has always been great at the market research stuff, and back then we did it all together. We figured my chances of making it in the music industry would be a lot better if I started a band."

"A Splinter of Moon?"

"No, not back then. My first band was called Gravel Road."

"Were you good?"

"Good enough, but that's all a first band really has to

be. I just wanted a group to play with, network, meet other local musicians. Find my people, you know?"

She opened the bag of blue corn chips, and popped one into her mouth. "Evan's dad has a lot of connections, and some genius ideas. I started Splinter six years ago, and he helped us gain momentum fast. The problem is touring."

"A couple of years until your lives are mostly yours again, right?"

"Sure," she agreed with a shrug. "And that's right around the time Evan will want to see his face on boxes of corn dogs."

"Really?"

"No, and he'd be pissed if he heard me say that, but you know what I mean."

"I'd be thrilled to have a restaurant half as busy as Señor Sushi."

"It's the most wonderfully inspiring and obnoxiously annoying thing about my husband. He's only satisfied when he's doing what no one else has, or what no one else can."

"Which parents did he get that from? Biological or adopted?"

"I do think Evan's drive comes from somewhere within. But his parents nurtured those qualities for sure."

"They seemed nice."

"Oh, they're great. Dorothy and Bill are always taking the kids to science museums, art shows, concerts and movies, interactive theater, animation festivals, improv workshops — you name it. They don't just believe in raising kids, they believe in cultivating their talents. Harmony still has movie nights with Grandpa, at least once a month. And Jazz plays tennis at the Austin Country Club with Grandma."

"You guys are members?"

"We're not, but they are. Bill does it for the contacts, but it isn't really our scene."

He looked down at the cutting board, chopping cabbage and concentrating on the vibrant shades of purple to prevent his joy for his brother from tipping into envy.

Klair took another handful of chips, then rolled the bag closed and pushed it toward Everett. "Take these, please. Don't let me have any more."

"One more margarita, and no more chips?"

"Sounds good," she agreed.

Half a margarita later, Klair had taken Everett on a brief tour of Evan's courtship of her, from *Wanna grab a cup of coffee?* to *Will you marry me?*

"How did he propose?" Everett asked.

"Oh my God … it was the most Evan thing ever."

"I'm not sure if that sounds like a good thing."

Klair laughed, reaching for the chips before snatching her hand back. "Evan had been like *crazy busy* for a while and he promised to take an afternoon off from work."

"Sounds familiar," Everett said to connect with Klair, not dig on his brother.

"Truth." She raised her glass, then took a sip and returned it to the counter. "He packed a picnic and we ate at the park. Meats and cheeses and two different bottles of wine. He had this amazing tiramisu made by his buddy, Alejandro. This was back in the days of yore, so people still read the paper. Right before dessert Evan asked me if I wanted to let our food settle and catch up on some current events. I thought it was weird, bringing a newspaper to our picnic, and even weirder to make a point of wanting to read it."

"He took out a full-page ad in the paper asking you to marry him?"

"That's exactly what he did," Klair said.

"Was it romantic?"

"*So romantic.*"

"Did you like it?"

"Oh my God, I loved it."

"So then, what's the problem? What makes it 'so Evan'?"

"No problem at the time. *At all.* It was later, when I found his checklist, and talked to Alejandro, and realized that he had a checklist to make sure he got a 'ten out of ten' proposal. Everything was planned, down to him being completely unavailable for the few weeks before our picnic. He wanted it so I would be craving his attention, and it would be easier for him to catch me off guard."

"So, wonderfully inspiring and obnoxiously annoying."

"Exactly." Klair smiled and took another sip.

Yet another story that could've made him feel like a failure, if he let it.

And that, Everett refused to do. It didn't matter that he had never even proposed to Clara. Three months after seeing the blue line on the white stick in the bathroom together, she finally had to say, "So, are you going to propose or what?"

Of course, he had *wanted* to. But Everett couldn't really afford a ring. Looking around and seeing the prices made him sad. *Next week for sure,* he kept telling himself, until the first trimester had expired and Clara made him feel like an asshole.

"Do I get to taste anything before Evan comes home?" she asked, once everything was done except for frying the fish.

"When is that?" Everett asked.

"Any minute now."

"I'll get to frying."

He nodded vaguely toward the living room, feeling almost comfortable.

The timing was perfect, with Everett finishing the last of the fish just ahead of Evan's arrival. But he didn't look in the mood to taste anything.

"What's wrong this time?" Klair asked as he entered the kitchen.

"I reached out to Blythe and Angelo, plus a bunch of other people who I thought might be able to help, but still no leads on a new station chef."

"Try this." Klair pushed a small plate toward him. One taco, covered in slaw and everything else, with a dollop of rice and a generous smear of guac.

Evan looked down at the plate. "Did you make this?"

"Everett made it."

Evan put the taco in his mouth. Then his eyes brightened with delight and surprise. He didn't say anything, just forked some rice into his mouth, took a second bite of taco, then swallowed it all.

"This is really great," he finally said.

"Don't sound so surprised." Klair slapped her man on the shoulder.

"I'm not ... it's just *really great.*"

"Thank you." This was what joy felt like. Everett wondered if he was blushing. "It's my mom's recipe."

Klair said, "I don't know if Rhett has to get back to California, but I still think you should take him up on his offer."

"I can stay," Everett offered, hoping that Evan would say yes. Staying would delay his plan to save Java Joe's, but doing so would still be worth it.

"You have restaurant experience, right?" Evan asked.

"Sure do." He owned a coffee shop, plus there was his

work study in college where he worked the cafeteria, plus that three months pulling the afternoon shift at Applebee's.

"And you're really fine staying out here for another few weeks?"

"I'll make a couple of calls."

"Well then," Evan said, extending his hand. "We might as well give it a try."

Everett shook it, feeling something coming to vibrant life inside him.

This was the beginning of everything he'd been dreaming of.

Chapter Twenty

TRAINING BEGAN THE FOLLOWING DAY, and it was even more brutal than Everett had imagined.

He'd known it wouldn't be easy. He'd seen what it was like to be in a busy kitchen on so many Food Network shows.

Evan had told him to be ready *no later than six,* so he'd set his alarm for five. Evan seemed both surprised and happy to see him when he knocked on the back door a few minutes early. He made them coffees in a French press, then they were on their way to Tequila Mockingbird.

"You'll be training with the senior station chef," Evan had said.

Everett couldn't wait. "What's he like?"

"I prefer you decide for yourself."

"Fair enough."

"One more thing," Evan said, keeping his eyes on the road. "In my kitchen, you'll address me as Chef. Bernardo too, since he's senior to you. Will that be a problem?"

"No, Chef!" Everett said cheerfully. He understood,

Evan couldn't afford to make the other staff jealous by revealing the twin bond that would undoubtedly develop.

When they got to the restaurant, Bernardo was waiting for them. Evan introduced Everett as Rhett, and told Bernardo to "make him useful." Then he left to start organizing some things in the walk-in, and Everett realized he wouldn't be shoulder-to-shoulder with his brother, but with Bernardo.

Not a problem. He would prove himself and earn the position.

So he didn't ask questions, watching the senior station chef instead and learning through observation.

Bernardo was in no way unkind, but he didn't waste a second on pleasantries.

Rhett, hand me the mallet.

Rhett, have you ever cooked with hatch chiles before?

Then once, nudging him to the side for a demonstration. *This is how you chop, Rhett.*

It shouldn't have mattered, but it was like Bernardo was running a cheese grater against his brain by constantly calling him the wrong name. He finally had to do something about it.

He leaned forward and whispered, "It's Everett, actually."

Bernardo couldn't have cared less. He turned, narrowed his eyes at Everett, then went back to beating his chicken breasts with the mallet.

He stayed silent after that, focusing on whatever task Bernardo assigned to him.

Bernardo somehow managed to get all of his work done while barely ever taking his eyes off of Everett. Soon, Evan joined them, barking orders and occasionally looking over his shoulder to check on his brother.

Seeing Evan in his element, where precision care and

passion appeared to permeate every decision, inspired Everett. He not only marveled at Evan's total control, Everett felt another flush of embarrassment thinking about how he had been handling things at Joe's. Everything Evan did made Everett feel like an amateur.

"Cooking in a professional kitchen is different than cooking at home." Bernardo often started his lessons by stating the obvious. "And what you are learning here is not unlike learning a language."

Everett kept chopping, wanting to look over at Bernardo, but acutely aware that the station chief needed him to keep going.

"The words are your ingredients. The more you use the language, the more you understand it, and the faster you can talk. Understand?"

"Yes, Chef."

"If we are making ceviche, then we need fresh fish, lemon or lime, chili peppers, chopped onions, salt, and coriander — yes?"

"Yes, Chef."

"Your recipes are like grammar. In a language, you need proper spelling and grammar to speak well and write well. Is it any different in the kitchen?"

"No, Chef."

"The better you understand vocabulary and grammar, the faster and more clearly you can speak. That is your job in this kitchen. Understand?"

"Yes, Chef."

"If you use the wrong words, then your meaning gets lost. The wrong ingredients make your dish a disaster." Bernardo paused just long enough to move his freshly sliced filets to the side. "What is the most important part of learning a new language, Everett?"

He wanted to cheer for the use of his proper name. "Knowing the right words?"

"Are you asking me or are you telling me?"

"Telling you," Everett guessed.

"That is *incorrect*. The most important part of learning a new language is *listening*. Are you a good listener, Everett?"

"I am." He hoped.

"When I came to this country, I did not know English. I was afraid to talk and worried that I would make too many mistakes. So I listened as much as I could. But only once I was willing to make mistakes did I discover what I didn't know. Does my English seem good to you, Everett?"

"Yes, Chef."

Bernardo stopped talking after that, except for the occasional barked order. But Everett watched everything he and Evan did.

Bernardo called him out on needing an extra few seconds to remember where the thyme was, and it felt like he wanted to put his hand in the garbage disposal when he blanked on the word for *chipotle*. Everett was trying his best, but he kept messing up, and Bernardo never seemed to let anything go.

But Evan's criticisms hurt more, because each time Everett messed up, Evan grew more agitated.

"*Like this.*" He took both the filet and the knife from Everett, then showed him the proper way to slice it. "You do it like that from now on if you want to stay."

And Everett realized that by volunteering to help, he might have put himself in the one situation that could destroy the delicate twin-bond that he'd been trying so hard to cultivate.

By mid-afternoon, the long day was catching up with

him. His knife felt heavier, the lights all seemed brighter, and the competing aromas somehow worked like a lullaby.

"RHETT!"

At first he thought his brother had shouted *RED*. Had he grabbed the wrong color of something? He started to panic, hot shame heating his cheeks like it had so many times since he donned his apron that morning. Then he decoded the bastardization of his name and blinked in embarrassment.

"Sorry, I—"

"What makes you think you can take a nap at your station?"

"I didn't think that."

"You're practically asleep. With a knife in your hand!"

"I'm sorry, Chef. I'm not used to getting up this early."

"Maybe it's because you're still on California time. Is that it, Rhett?"

"No, Chef."

"What time are you on?"

"I'm on Austin time."

"No, Rhett. You're on *my time.*"

"I can do better, Chef."

"Better than falling asleep while you're cutting fish? I should fucking hope so."

Evan turned away, shaking his head in disgust. Everett reminded himself that it wasn't personal. Or maybe it was personal, but it was tough love, like on *Kitchen Nightmares*.

That thought led him to Jimi, then to Clara. He was sorry that she'd probably had to leave Jimi with her mother, and hoped that her audition had gone well.

But then he realized that he'd allowed his focus to wander. He wrestled it back, determined that this time he wouldn't let it go.

The room found its rhythm, and for the first time it felt like Everett was a part of the flow. Bernardo even threw a smile his way. He wanted to strike up a conversation, maybe ask a question or drop a comment, but he was afraid to break the cadence or get something wrong.

But Evan's scowl deepened, even though Everett was doing better, until he finally stomped out of the kitchen.

Bernardo turned to Everett. "Don't worry. Believe it or not, you're doing better than the last guy."

"Are you serious?"

"You have not cried yet."

"*Yet?* The other guy cried?"

"Si." Bernardo frowned. "He sounded like a butchered cat."

"How long did he last?"

"Until he started crying."

Everett gestured toward the door, meaning his brother. "So, I guess he's just always like that?"

"Chef is one of those men who can build a house on a boulder."

"I'm not sure what that means," Everett admitted.

"He doesn't give up. We stand at our stations and we do our work no matter what comes at us. But Chef," Bernardo tapped his temple, "he does everything. So we do everything we can for him."

Then Bernardo went back to work.

Everett was exhausted, but he pushed himself to work harder. If his identical twin could do it, then Everett had no excuses. He could no longer allow himself to be a failure either.

When he tugged off his apron at the end of the day, everything ached, from his neck to his very sore feet.

He turned to Bernardo. "I'm not going to quit."

"I'm glad to hear that." A simple nod.

"You think I can do this? Tell me honestly."

"Honestly?" Bernardo shrugged with an apologetic frown. "No."

But that just made Everett more determined.

Chapter Twenty-One

EVAN SAID nothing on the drive back to his house, and Everett was afraid that even small talk would worsen his brother's mood. He couldn't face a family dinner where Klair asked how his first day had been — and maybe started a fight with Evan if he didn't gush about how well Everett was doing.

So, as soon as Evan parked in the driveway, Everett excused himself by claiming a headache and headed straight to the guest house. He fell asleep minutes after walking in, but then woke up rather unfortunately at four in the morning, unable to stop thinking.

Bernardo didn't think he could make it. Was he trying to inspire Everett by being hard on him? Or should Everett quit before he did so much damage to his relationship with Evan that their twin bond would never recover?

His anxiety continued to spiral until it was time to take another silent ride with Evan, back to Tequila Mockingbird, for his second day of training.

He got a "good luck" from Evan before they entered, then his brother left him with Bernardo.

His phone rang. *Clara.*

It was three in the morning for her. He didn't want to answer, but he was afraid it was an emergency. Maybe something had happened to Jimi.

He held up a finger to Bernardo — *one second* — then took the call. "I can't talk—"

"Then why did you answer your phone? I know how to leave a message."

"I've been accused of not returning my voicemails … or remembering that I got them."

"Would you like me to call you back?" Clara sounded uncharacteristically chipper.

"Just tell me what's up. Quickly."

She squealed into the phone. "Oh my God, Everett! I got the gig!"

"Congratulations, really. I couldn't be happier for you." An apologetic glance at Bernardo, his eyes pleading for another moment. "So, what does that mean?"

"I'll be touring in the fall, so I'd love for you to take Jimi full-time. Starting in the new school year, through Christmas vacation."

"Are you kidding? That would be great!"

Everett could hear the smile in her voice. "I'm thrilled to know you feel that way."

"I've really gotta go."

"Cool. We're still on for this weekend, right?"

"What's this weekend?" Everett asked.

"You mean, other than the fact that it's *your* weekend?"

"But I told you that I was in Texas."

"Are you telling me that you're still not going to be back in time for this weekend? What the hell, Everett?"

"I got tied up."

"That's not an explanation!"

"I'm helping my brother open a restaurant." Everett

cleared his throat, casting a glance at Bernardo. "I'll be here for a month."

Back to her usual anger: "And you're just now telling me?"

"Can we talk about this later?"

"Fuck you, Everett."

Don't swear at me! "I'm at work."

"Right, at your brother's restaurant. This is still the brother you met last week, or did you find another one?"

"Come on, Clara …"

"Come on, nothing, Everett. This is total bullshit. The *opposite* of what you promised me."

"I can still take Jimi all fall."

"Oh, wow. Thank you! It's so gracious of you to do the bare minimum asked of you."

Bernardo was now glaring at Everett, the patience all gone from his eyes. He gestured: two aggressive fingers cutting his own throat.

"Clara, I really have to—"

"I scheduled another trip to Nashville this weekend, based on your agreement to take care of your son. I should have known you would pull this crap again."

Everett opened his mouth to respond just as Evan entered the kitchen.

Evan looked at his brother holding the phone, then to the station chief.

Bernardo shrugged, frowning with a sad little shake of his head.

"You have seriously got to be kidding me," Evan said. "Are you making a personal call right now?"

Everett covered the mouthpiece and turned to his brother. "*Taking* one, sorry. It's my ex-wife. She's calling with an emergency."

"Who are you talking to?" Clara asked.

"I really have to go. I promise, we can talk about all of this later. You're not wrong about any of it. And I swear I'm not trying to blow you off."

"Convenient. Because that's exactly what you're doing."

"Get off the goddamn phone, Everett," Evan said.

"Don't you hang up on me!" Clara yelled.

Everett had a great idea, if he could only manage to get it out of his mouth. With fire in his throat, he gurgled, "I'll be right back!" to Evan and Bernardo.

Then he scurried through the kitchen and exploded through the rear door.

Outside, he said, "Listen, why don't you fly out here before you go to Nashville? There's a direct flight to Austin from Las Orillas."

"No, I'm not making things easy on you by flying to Austin. Fuck you, Evan."

"STOP SWEARING AT ME!"

Clara didn't respond.

"I'm not trying to make this easier for *me*, Clara. I'm trying to solve the problem. I can stay with Jimi. He can meet his Uncle Evan and his Aunt Klair. He has two cousins now, Harmony and Jazz."

"No, Everett."

"Why?"

"I'd rather leave Jimi with my mother, *again*, than fly out to Austin and leave him with strangers."

"They're not strangers, they're family you haven't met yet. Besides, I'm the one you would be leaving him with."

"Really? Because I thought you were busy helping your brother open a restaurant."

"Hold on—"

The back door opened and Bernardo's head appeared

in the doorway. "You remember that question you asked me at the end of your shift?"

"I know, I know," Everett said.

"I hope so." Bernardo slammed the door.

"You know what?" Clara asked.

"I *really* have to go." But of course, there was no way she was about to let him hang up in the middle of her shit fit.

"I have a counter idea, Everett. Would you like to hear it?"

Just hang up. You can make things right later.

"Is it serious? Or is this going to be one of your—"

"How about we go ahead and do that — I'll send Jimi to Austin, but no need for me to come with him. I appreciate how much you're trying to help me, so I'm going to go ahead and take full advantage of that and send him on a plane all by himself."

"Okay, so—"

"No reason to pick him back up immediately, right? You've got this. I'll leave him there with you, and maybe I can start actually getting some shit done in my life. Sound good?"

Hang. Up.

He didn't kill the call, nor did he answer. Doing so would only encourage Clara further. Not that she needed any more encouragement than she already had.

"We might as well take him out of school. No reason he should be going to class when he can hang out with his new family in Texas."

"Sorry I made the suggestion. Can we please pick this up later?"

"So you're really doing this?"

"If you mean honoring my commitment to help open this restaurant, then yes, that's what I'm doing."

"I cannot fucking believe you."

"I'm sorry that any of this is hard on you."

"It's not that it's hard on me, Everett. It's that I can't believe I was ever married to such a man-child."

"I'm a man-child for trying to give my child a better life?"

"I seriously don't understand how your brain works. Explain how you opening a restaurant for your brother in Austin will give Jimi a better life? Your son needs you here, in Las Orillas, now. You haven't seen him for weeks."

"My mother died!"

"And then you took an unscheduled road trip."

"Look, Clara. I've gotta go. If I was in Las Orillas right now, of course I would love to take Jimi. Once I'm back in town, I'll bend over backwards to make everything right with you, and with him. But I'm here right now, and I need to finish what I started."

The back door opened, but this time it wasn't Bernardo.

"What the hell are you still doing out here, Rhett?"

Evan's expression said he'd heard everything, and Everett flooded with shame. His argument with Clara was more evidence that he was an inferior copy of Evan.

"Is that your brother?" Then Clara yelled, "Tell him I said *hi*!"

"Bernardo is waiting on you."

"I've gotta go."

"When are you going to call me back?" Clara demanded.

"Tonight," Everett said.

He hung up the phone, dropped it into his pocket, and turned to his brother. "I'm sorry, Chef. That was my ex-wife. She was having an emergency with our son."

Evan's expression remained hard, but he asked, "Is everything okay?"

"Yes, Chef. We just had to work it out."

"And did you?"

"Yes, Chef."

"It's better if you go now than later. You understand that, right? Training you is expensive."

You haven't even offered to pay me.

"If this isn't going to work out, I need to know now."

Way to say thank you.

"It's going to work out."

"I hope so."

"You better not make me look like an asshole," Evan said, holding the back door open for his brother.

It took everything Everett had to nod and say, "Thank you, Chef."

Chapter Twenty-Two

ONCE INSIDE, Everett washed his hands and got to work.

Despite the argument with Clara, he managed to focus without fucking up for the next few hours.

When they finally took a five-minute break, he texted: *I'm sorry about all of that. I promise to call you back. Soon as I can.* Followed by a barrage of emojis and a *Please tell Jimi that I love and miss him. I'll see you both soon.*

Everett wasn't sure if he was doing better, or if Evan was taking it easy on him because he felt sorry for his fight with Clara.

But Bernardo seemed pleased. Maybe Everett was actually doing a decent job.

The day finally seemed to be going well. Despite a rocky start, it might end up being his best one in Austin so far. By lunchtime, Everett was certain that he'd seen Evan smile, and felt even surer that the smile had been on account of him.

But then Evan got a text that stripped the smile off his face.

And for the rest of the day, Everett was back in hell.

. . .

EVAN'S bad mood continued through the drive home. As soon as the car was parked, he turned to Everett and said, "See ya."

He didn't dare follow Evan inside, so he went straight to the guest house again.

He called Clara, but she didn't answer. Should he leave a voicemail? He decided to text another apology. Maybe once she'd cooled off, she'd be more open to talking about sending Jimi out.

Except — maybe she was right. If Jimi was here, Everett would barely see him in the evenings. And he was already imposing on Evan and Klair by being here himself. It wouldn't be fair to dump Jimi on Klair after school. He couldn't afford a sitter, either, since he was basically working for room and board.

He simply didn't have the resources to be a good father right now, and that realization made him feel like a maggot.

He didn't even know if he was invited to dinner. How could he assume that Jimi would be welcome?

He was going to be here for a month, until Gabriel's leg finished healing. Surely that meant he should be taking more responsibility for himself. He had his own place, with a kitchenette. If Klair kept him in groceries, then why wouldn't he cook for himself?

It was costing a fortune to stay in Austin. Financially, emotionally, and — *oh shit*, he *really* needed to return the Mustang. Even if he wasn't getting rides to and from work, it might be cheaper to take a FASTr wherever he needed to go without Evan.

No, this train of thought was taking him back to self-pity. He should offer to cook for the family, even though the last thing he wanted right now was to spend any more time in the kitchen. If Klair accepted his offer, that made him more like family. And if she insisted on feeding him instead, that was more proof that he was already part of the family. It would be a win for Everett either way.

He went to the back door, and quietly entered without knocking. Less like a houseguest than a member of the family. Or maybe like an indentured servant who had earned his run of the house.

But something was wrong, and Everett could feel it immediately. Had Evan's text been the harbinger of an emergency? Or was this another round in his ongoing battle with Klair?

Jazz broke the silence just as Everett was rounding the corner into the living room, where Evan and Klair were standing with crossed arms in front of their son, a pair of stars in a separate constellation.

Evan stepped back out of sight before either of them caught sight of him.

"You keep saying this is my fault, but it's not my fault!"

Klair said, "Neither of us have used that word even once. We're not assigning *fault* to anyone, Jazz. We're saying that there are things we do and do not allow in this house — with no exceptions."

"But—"

"We're done discussing this." Evan pointed toward the stairs. "Go to your room. We'll talk later."

Jazz just stormed by him in a huff, heading outside instead of upstairs like he'd been told.

Everett was about to retreat back to the guest house when Evan turned on Klair. He should have gone, but now he couldn't move.

"How could you let this happen?"

"What?" Klair wasn't loud, but she sounded furious.

"How many fights is this now? Four?"

Four. Everett only knew about the one.

"Yes, Evan. Four fights. And guess how many we would have if you were actually ever home?"

"It's somehow *my fault* that Jazz is getting into fights at school?"

"You seriously can't see that? Jazz is acting out because you're not around to be the father he—"

"No way, Klair. You can't put this on me. We both know he takes after your side of the family. I never got into fights at school, not even one. But your brothers did *all the time.*"

That was a low blow. Exactly the kind of thing Everett would say to Clara, back in the early days of their divorce. Before the Ds told him to knock that shit off, because Jimi could overhear and take it to heart.

He shouldn't be listening to any of this.

Everett was afraid to retreat and risk being heard. But he couldn't stand here frozen forever. Jazz might come back inside, or Harmony could come downstairs. Either Evan or Klair could move a few feet and blow his cover. It wouldn't look good if they thought he was spying on him.

He gathered his courage and turned to go, tiptoeing like he was five and he had to make it to his bedroom before Marco and Roberto realized he was home from the library.

He made it outside without being noticed. But instead of returning to the guest house, he joined Jazz at the pool.

"Hey," Everett said, taking a seat.

"Hey." But that was it.

They sat in silence for five minutes or so. But he wasn't in a hurry, happy to sit in his chair for however long it took the kid to open up. He'd been in similar situations, plenty of times. He had a decent idea around what Jazz might be going through right now. Probably better than either one of his parents.

Jazz wouldn't want to be pushed.

"You don't have to babysit me," Jazz finally said, nodding toward the guest house.

"I'm not babysitting you. I like it out here. It's relaxing, looking at the pool."

"Like you would be out here if I wasn't."

"I might be."

"Yeah, right." Jazz crossed his arms, said nothing for several long seconds, then, "They act like I want to fight."

"I know."

Jazz looked over at Everett, surprised. "It's not my fault."

"I know."

"Well, someone should tell *them.*"

"Why don't you tell me what actually happened?"

More silence, a minute or so this time, then, "Isaiah and Aiden keep backing me into a corner. I'd run if I could."

"I heard about Isaiah, who's Aiden?"

"A total fucking asshole, that's who."

"Okay." Everett laughed. "Can you be more specific?"

"Aiden goes to my school, but he also used to be in Scouts."

"Were you guys friends then?"

"NO." Jazz shook his head furiously. "Aiden doesn't really have any friends, but a lot of kids pretend that they like him because his dad's the troop leader. He's the reason I stopped going to Boy Scouts."

"What kinds of things did he do?"

"Call me names and make up stories about me. One time, he hid my book. It had all my merit badge stuff in it. I knew it was him, but he kept denying it. He told his dad that I was just blaming it on him because I didn't want to admit that I'd lost it."

"Did you ever say anything mean to him?"

"No."

"Really?" Everett looked at Jazz. "Not even *once*? It's really *all* him?"

Jazz went stony-faced, and Everett knew that he'd pushed too soon.

"Did your parents know what Aiden was doing?"

"No. I said I wanted more time for my homework because high school was harder than eighth grade. But really, I just hated seeing Aiden."

"And you've known Isaiah since eighth grade?"

Jazz nodded. "He used to take whatever he wanted from my lunch. He said it was a nerd tax. When I finally told him no a few weeks ago, he punched me."

"Have you told your parents any of this?"

"What's the point? They've already made up their minds."

He gave the accusation a few seconds to sit. Jazz needed to feel like Everett was on his side.

"How did you get your brothers to stop beating on you?"

"I never really did," Everett admitted. "I just got old enough to move out. And now that we're all adults, it would be assault if they hit me."

"Is this supposed to cheer me up?"

"Maybe it can, if you look at things the right way."

"And what way is that?" Jazz asked.

"Understand that it's *them*, not *you*. Aiden and Isaiah are doing what they're doing because they're the ones who are fucked up."

Jazz didn't respond, but he seemed to be thinking rather than pouting.

They both had their eyes on the pool, staring at the glittering, rippling water for another few minutes before Jazz finally spoke.

"I should get inside."

"You mean, up to your room, before they realize you didn't go there in the first place?"

Jazz smiled. "Yeah."

"Go on. Your secret's safe with me."

The kid made it two steps, then turned back to Everett.

"Thanks, Rhett. I'm glad you're here."

"You're welcome." He hated the name, but the rest of it felt like sun on his shoulders.

Everett stayed by the pool, staring at the water. If Jimi was being bullied, would he know? He barely saw the kid and he used video games to avoid the real parenting. Even if Jimi wasn't trying to keep it a secret, the old Everett probably wouldn't have noticed the signs.

He was starting to see Clara's point.

"This seat taken?"

Everett was yanked out of his thoughts. He looked up to see his twin brother smiling awkwardly.

"Please." He gestured to the seat beside him.

"Sorry you had to see that." Evan's voice was softer than usual once he finally spoke. Down but not defeated. "Things have just been … tense."

"You have a lot going on. Opening Tequila would be hard enough without all the stuff at home, right?" Everett paused, then decided to say it bluntly. "And my being here can't be helping the situation."

Evan gave him a tired smile. "This has nothing to do with you. If anything, you're trying to help."

It was a wonderful thing to hear, even if Evan was only being kind.

"Klair and I go through phases. Always have. We'll go

a year without disagreeing about anything more than what to watch, then three miserable months where it feels like neither of us can say anything right."

"Is it always about how much you're working?"

"Pretty much. I almost postponed opening Tequila another year, I was dreading the fighting so much. And everything has taken longer and been harder than I'd expected."

"Why didn't you postpone?"

"Everything lined up at once — the investors, the perfect space, a major competitor suddenly declaring bank-ruptcy. Everything seemed to be saying, *it's time.*"

"Except Klair wasn't saying it, was she?"

Evan sighed. "We've done this before, and it believe it or not, things were much harder the first time. Harmony and Jazz were both under ten when we opened Señor. Klair had to do all of the heavy lifting at home back then. But our lives aren't as complicated now. The kids are old enough to do their own thing for the most part."

Evan stopped. Said nothing for thirty seconds or so. Then, "I could use a beer. You want one?"

"That sounds great."

Evan was already back on his feet and walking toward the house.

Everett wasn't sure what to say. He understood where Evan was coming from, yet he couldn't help feeling that Klair had a point. Sure, Harmony and Jazz might be old enough to be doing their own thing, but Jazz was still coming home with black eyes and bloody noses, and Harmony seemed like she had been unplugged from the family for a while.

Evan handed him an open beer, then sat and took a long swallow.

Everett sipped his. "This is delicious. I've never tasted beer like this before."

"It's brewed here in Austin, and we'll be selling it at Tequila."

"Is that ... pecan?"

Evan looked over, seeming impressed. "It's a full-bodied malty porter with locally grown pecans. From an area full of cedar and mesquite."

"Interesting."

"Point is," Evan picked up from where he'd left off before going to fetch their beers, "I'm doing it all for them. That's what I want Klair to realize — that it will all be worth it once Tequila takes off."

How many times had Everett said the same thing to Clara?

"I used to have the same fight with my ex. Señor's is a billion times busier than my place, but the argument was still the same. I was spending too much time at the restaurant, or coffee shop if I'm being honest ..." An embarrassed laugh before he continued. "I kept telling myself that I'd be in better shape next month, and then I could spend more time with Clara and Jimi. But I never got there."

"That sucks." Evan shook his head. "It must be really hard to raise a kid when you're not together."

"I hate it," Everett admitted.

"Do you guys get along? You and Clara, I mean."

"We fight all the time. But never in front of Jimi."

"That's good," Evan said.

"It's weird, there's still a lot of love and respect there, she just doesn't like some of the choices I've made in my life." And he couldn't help agreeing with her.

Evan said nothing, just listened.

After another swallow, Everett continued. "She's right.

Jimi is seven now, and growing up so fast. Half the time I feel like I've already missed most of his childhood."

"If you could do it differently, what would you change?"

"The way I handled Java Joe's. I should have taken some bigger risks and done things right. Or found some other way to make money, so I didn't lose out on my life with Jimi and Clara." Everett took a long swallow — he needed a moment to get ahead of the emotions that threatened to make his voice crack. "I miss them both so much, and the place still isn't even breaking even."

"That's the worst …" Evan shook his head. "Working yourself to exhaustion and still feeling like you've done a shit job."

Everett turned to his brother. "Are you kidding? I get wanting to do better no matter what, but how could you *ever* feel like you're doing a shit job? Your restaurant is amazing. You have everything to be proud about."

"Thanks for saying that, but head shit is head shit. You're always feeling like you should do more and that success is just around the next corner, right?"

"Yeah," Everett agreed.

"I think the same is true for every successful entrepreneur."

"But you already have a successful restaurant," Everett said.

"Sure. But do you know how many successful restaurants can start failing overnight? This is Austin, there are great places to eat everywhere. I have to stay on top, pay attention, work harder than the next guy … what is it, why the face?"

Everett gave his brother a sad little laugh. "My landlord said almost the same exact thing."

"This the landlord that was raising your 'friend's'

rent?"

"Yeah," Everett admitted.

"So have you figured out a way to make that work?"

"I will. But honestly, right now I'm more concerned about making things right with Clara and Jimi. She's really excited about her new gig, but I can't be available to take Jimi right now."

"Because you're here?"

"Yes, but I really want to be."

After another swig, Evan asked, "Could Jimi come out to Austin?"

"I offered, but Clara hated the idea."

"How hard did you try?"

"Hard enough to get yelled at." Everett laughed, but now it was awkward.

"Maybe you should try again. Don't assume that you've lost the argument just because the first round didn't go your way."

"I will." Everett took the last swallow of his beer. "I promise."

"Just like that?"

"Just like that," Everett repeated. "I need to challenge my own assumptions more."

"We all do."

"Yeah, but you're ahead of me there, brother. That's why you're living in the big house and I'm kicking it in a shack by the pool."

"You'll have your own big house one day." Evan smiled. "It's in the DNA, right?"

"I sure as hell hope so."

They shared another several moments of silence, and Everett couldn't remember the last time he felt more at peace. Regardless of what happened when he called Clara, he now had this connection to his brother, and that was a significant victory.

Evan stood and picked up Everett's empty bottle from the ground. "Dinner in a half hour?"

Everett smiled. "Sounds great. That gives me some time to make a phone call."

Evan gave his brother a knowing nod, then turned around and started toward the house.

But Everett had to admit he was relieved when Clara didn't answer. He would try again after dinner.

Everett sighed, then he sat on the couch and stared at the TV, keeping his eyes on all of the nothing until it was finally time for dinner, hoping to his soul that he didn't do anything stupid to blow it.

Chapter Twenty-Three

DINNER WAS QUIET. Jazz chose to eat in his room, Harmony was out with friends, and Klair seemed distracted. Or maybe embarrassed?

But the pulled-pork sandwiches and spinach salad were the perfect accompaniment for Evan's questions about Everett's childhood. He stuck mostly to happy memories of Mom and the dishes she'd taught him to cook, for Klair's sake.

When the meal was over, Everett felt fortified. He could have a reasonable conversation with Clara, and he wouldn't lose his temper. He would find a way to be there for her and Jimi without letting Evan down.

But what if she didn't answer? She still hadn't responded to his last voicemail. Maybe Clara was more pissed at him than he realized. Maybe—

"Hey, Everett," she said after the second ring, sounding neither angry nor happy to hear from him.

"Hey!" His mind went totally blank. For an excruciating moment, there was absolutely nothing in it. But then he cleared his throat and found himself. "I'm glad you answered … I wanted to talk."

"About what?" Now she sounded distant, bordering on cold.

"Anything. I just wanted to connect."

Clara sighed without replying.

"Is it wrong that I called?" Everett asked.

"I don't know if *wrong* is the right word … maybe *rude* is better?"

"It's rude to call you now?"

"No. It's rude to call me with nothing to say."

"I just wanted to connect before I asked you—"

"We're connected. Now tell me what you want before I hang up."

Everett had told Evan he would try harder, but what if no amount of trying would be enough?

"I was hoping we could revisit the conversation about Jimi coming out to Austin."

"You want to hear me say *NO* again?"

"I want you to be reasonable. I have family out here now, which means Jimi has family out here now. It's perfectly reasonable for me to want us all to meet."

"I'm sure he'll meet them someday. But it's not happening now."

"Why are you so mad at me?" Everett asked.

"Have you checked your email today?"

"No. Why?"

"I've filed papers with the court requesting full custody. You should have received a copy in email. You need to sign the forms and send them back."

"Full custody!"

"Full custody. These are digital signatures. A couple of clicks and you're done. You should be able to manage it, even with your very busy schedule helping your brand new brother in Texas."

"Why are you doing this?"

"The fact that you're even asking me why I'm doing this is *why I'm doing this.*"

"What's that supposed to mean?" He stopped pacing and flopped back onto the couch.

"It means that we've had this conversation too many times for us to have it again right now."

"Why can't you see how hard I'm trying?"

"I can see exactly how hard you're trying, Everett. That's precisely the point."

It took everything inside him not to yell. "But I *am* trying."

"All the way from Texas, too. Amazing job."

"I just need to finish up here, then I'm full-time dad. I can even take him before the fall. Okay, Clara? You don't have to threaten me."

"This isn't a threat," she said in her most stone-cold voice so far. "This is happening, Everett."

"You can't do this. I have rights, as his father."

"Yes you do, Everett. And no one is trying to take any of your rights away, especially me. But it's clear that you don't really have any genuine interest in being part of Jimi's life."

"OF COURSE I—"

"I'm talking." Clara didn't raise her voice, but she didn't need to; the one she was using had ripped into his response like a knife through paper. "You see Jimi as a reflection of you, and he needs to fit into your life."

"That's not true!"

"It *is* true. And until you recognize that you're doing it, the two of us will continue to have very regular conflict."

How could he reset the conversation?

"I see how unfair I've been in asking you to pick up my slack. But I've changed. I'm ready to step up. It isn't fair for you to focus on my old patterns instead of seeing this new situation for what it is."

"What is it I'm not seeing, Everett?"

"You're not seeing that Jimi has family out here."

"A family that didn't give a shit about you or him two weeks ago. You can be such a stupid asshole sometimes." Then: "GODDAMIT."

Surprisingly, Everett felt calmer than usual in the face of Clara's anger. "Finding my true family has grounded me. It's the connection that's been missing my whole life. You understand that, right?"

"Sure, Everett. I understand."

"Then why do you keep talking to me like a robot?"

"Because you're not getting it. If I don't talk to you like this, I'll yell at you. I can't help it."

"How many times have you told me to grow up, Clara? That's what I'm doing."

"Even if you call it 'growing,' you're still putting Everett first."

"So that I can be a better father. Then we won't need to change the custody agreement."

"I'm moving to Tennessee, and I'm taking Jimi with me. Unless you plan on moving too, joint custody no longer makes sense."

"You're moving to Tennessee?"

"Yes. To Nashville."

Everett was crushed. Things would never be the same again and he felt it down to his toenails. "For a gig."

No response.

"I'm just asking … if you're moving to Nashville and you're going to be playing all the time, who will be watching Jimi?"

"You're in *Texas*, Everett. And you know who I'm going to leave Jimi with?" She waited a beat in case he had an answer, but he didn't so she finished. "With someone more responsible than you. *That's who.*"

Then she hung up.

Chapter Twenty-Four

TODAY WAS Everett's trial by fire — instead of training at the empty Tequila Mockingbird, he would be working the lunch shift at Señor Sushi. And instead of Bernardo, who would assist Evan on entrees, Everett would be preparing appetizers and sauces under the supervision of Morris, a short, wiry man with a goatee and elaborate tattoos peeking out from the pristine white cuffs of his chef's coat.

All he had to do was focus on assisting Evan and Morris in making unfamiliar dishes while trying not to think about the fact that Clara might shut him out of Jimi's life for good.

No pressure.

"Listen up, bitch, I'mma tell you again, but this time you need to listen, because if Chef yells at me, you're going to wish you were dead." Morris pointed at the dish, that was apparently full of enough mistakes to inspire suicide.

Jimi is moving to Tennessee and you may never see him.

"You get what I'm saying, bitch?" Morris finished. He

never meant the word as an insult; *bitch* was just one of his favorite things to say.

"I get you, Chef." But really, Everett had no idea what he'd done wrong. Because all he could think about was losing his son before he'd had a chance to be a good father.

He shoved that thought aside. He would have plenty of time to think about them later (like any of the countless times he would be alone in his future life). Right now he should be thinking about only one thing: the fajita egg rolls he was supposed to be frying.

Plus whatever Morris had just told him, of course.

"That's what I'm talking about, bitch!" Morris sounded excited, and even took a moment to clap him on his shoulder. "Now get on that chipotle dipping sauce. We're almost out."

Everett turned to face the stove behind him and began to read the dipping sauce recipe, adding ingredients to a fresh sauce pot as he went.

"So you ready for the lunch rush?" Morris didn't wait for an answer. "Because this bitch is about to heat up."

"Ready, Chef."

Morris pointed to the mounted screen in between them, displaying and categorizing customer orders as they came in. "You're on the Tex-Mex dumplings."

"I've got the Tex-Mex dumplings," Everett repeated with a nod.

The conversation went quiet after that, until Everett finished his first batch of potstickers, stuffed with ground beef, black beans, corn cilantro, chunked and grated jalapeño, and a dollop of sour cream to moisten it, plus another drop of what the Señor Sushi kitchen called *fire sauce*.

"Another batch, and pinch the top tighter next time,"

Morris said as he examined Everett's work. "This one's probably going to fall apart in the pan."

Everett started on his second batch of dumplings.

"Those are great." Morris nodded in approval as he put the first one into the pan that Morris was tending.

"Don't I get a *bitch*?" Everett laughed.

"I decide when you've earned it, bitch."

Morris gave him two more compliments before Everett was wrenched violently away from the rhythm he'd worked to establish.

The kitchen fell entirely silent. Everett hadn't heard the initial question, but by the way Sierra — the nicest of all the servers he had met so far — stared at Evan in fear, something had gone horribly wrong.

Evan finally spoke. "Tell me *exactly* what he said. I won't be pissed at you. Nothing *he* said is *your* fault. Do you understand that, Sierra?"

"Yes." She nodded. "I do."

"So what did he say?"

A sigh, then: "He said he couldn't believe he was being charged five-star prices for the pig slop we're serving."

The expression on Evan's face — shockingly — suggested that he might have been expecting something much worse. "Which slop in particular?"

"You mean, what did he order?"

"Yes, Sierra. What did he order?"

"He was complaining about his appetizer. Tex-Mex dumplings."

Everett's heart went cold. Had he done something wrong with the last batch that Morris hadn't caught?

Only his third day, and he might have ruined Evan's reputation for good.

"Bring him back," Evan said.

Then Sierra was off and the staff pretended like they

weren't fully distracted for the next minute or so until she led the amateur critic into the kitchen.

Evan had his arms crossed, standing between the kitchen door and his staff. "You had a complaint about your meal?"

"Are you the one who made my dumplings?"

"This is my restaurant."

Everett braced himself. He gotten enough glimpses of Evan's temper to know that his brother could be terrifying if provoked.

"I'm sorry you didn't enjoy your meal," Evan said evenly. "Can you please tell me what the problem was?"

PLEASE ... Was he serious?

"The problem is you're charging eighteen dollars for a dollar's worth of potstickers."

"So it's the price you have a problem with."

"That. And the dogfood taste. If I wanted to be fed crap, I'd eat at Applebee's. But at least they get the plating right."

"Ah." Evan nodded. "So there was also a problem with the plating."

"Not if you've got kindergartners making the potstickers back here. In that case I applaud you for teaching the little tikes a work ethic early. But I suggest getting rid of the fat-fingered one who made these. One of the dumplings had split open. It was basically an empty noodle. Nah-ah," he shook his head, "not for twenty dollars. Fuck that."

Eighteen dollars.

"Understood. You didn't feel like you got what you paid for."

"I haven't paid yet." The asshole laughed to himself.

"I would offer you a meal on the house, but we both

know that wouldn't get either of us anywhere. Are you dining with friends this afternoon?"

He snorted. "Unfortunately, this place was *my* recommendation."

Evan nodded. "Then you have a choice. You can stay and remain on your best behavior, or you can leave and I will be happy to cover the cost of your friends' meal. In both scenarios you are never welcome in this establishment again."

"Because I don't like your shitty food?"

"No. Because you're rude and insulting, and not the kind of customer we cater to."

"At a restaurant called Señor Sushi?" He laughed like the name was offensive.

"Yes," Evan nodded, still holding his stare. "Exactly."

Then he said nothing, waiting for the asshole to make his move.

"You're not going to take responsibility for my fucked-up dumpling?"

Evan nodded again. "I offered to cover the meal for your entire table."

"If I go."

"That's right." Another nod. "If you go."

"What about my food?"

"I suggest you not order anything else. I'm quite sure that we will be unable to satisfy your—"

"Don't talk to me like I'm the problem here, buddy."

"You're welcome to leave now and never come back. If you stay, I will make sure that the appetizers are not on your bill, but you'll pay for the rest of your meal."

"You're a real asshole, you know that?" the asshole said.

"My restaurant, my rules."

Everett expected the dickhead to blow up, but instead

he spun around in a huff and marched back into the dining room. The entire kitchen finally seemed to exhale, with everyone scurrying back to work at once, except for Everett who was making his way over to Evan with an apology turning in his mind.

"I'm so—"

"Don't worry about it." Evan shook his head, raising a hand to stop him. "That guy's a jerk, and he cost us too much time already. We've got other customers to serve."

"I'm right back at it, I promise, Chef. I just wanted to say sorry for screwing up."

Evan sighed, then spent a few moments he couldn't afford to help his brother understand. "The only thing that guy managed to do was make himself look like a major cock in front of everyone. Even his friends know who he is, and he knows they know it. His issue was obviously about the prices, and that's certainly not on you."

Relief flooded his body, so deep that Everett could feel it in the tips of his fingers.

"But what *is* on you," Evan continued, "is the shape of those dumplings. Did you follow the recipe exactly?"

"Yes, Chef."

"Could one or more of your dumplings have left this kitchen broken?"

"Yes, Chef?"

"Then that's on you, or Sierra, or you and Sierra. Get it right next time and we're good."

Evan turned back around and started working.

Morris was laughing to himself when Everett returned to his station.

"Chef made that bitch look like a little bitch," he said.

And Everett knew exactly what he meant.

Chapter Twenty-Five

ANOTHER DAY, another silent ride home. While Evan steeped in his thoughts, Everett kept coming back to the phone call with Clara. The custody papers. Nashville. Never seeing Jimi again. He couldn't see a solution to it, and he couldn't stop thinking about it until he did.

By the time he was alone in the guest house, he realized that he had nothing clean to wear to work tomorrow. It was time to gather up the pile of dirty clothes in the corner and find the washing machine.

Klair must have had the same thought, because there was an empty basket sitting on the floor beside the couch.

He gathered his dirty clothes, then headed toward the main house to see if anyone might want to rap out before dinner.

No one in the living room, so Everett went into the kitchen. But it was empty, too.

He was hoping to see someone before starting his load, just in case someone else was planning on doing some laundry at the same time. Plus, he wasn't even sure where the washer and dryer were.

He went back into the living room and found Harmony marching through it. She frowned at him and announced: "Be careful. Mom is on the warpath."

"We were having a conversation, young lady!" Klair snapped as she emerged from the hallway. "You don't get to walk away from me."

Harmony ignored her mother, saying to Everett: "You know it's serious when she calls me *young lady*. But it's also kind of exciting. I used to get in trouble sometimes just so I could hear it."

"Nobody's in the mood for your sarcasm right now …"

"You were going to say 'young lady' just now, weren't you?" Harmony taunted her mother. "You had to stop yourself."

"Get back up to your room and start studying—"

"Or what, Mom? What's going to happen if I don't?"

"Then you're going to fail *another test* and—"

"Another test that only you care about!"

"I'm not the only one who cares about your failed tests, young lady."

Harmony turned from Klair to him. "*See.*"

Everett had assumed that Harmony was a straight-A student, because she was always in her room, 'doing her homework.' It hadn't occurred to him that she might be spending so much time studying because she was struggling.

"You used to be on track for valedictorian."

"I also used to be obsessed with balloon animals. So yeah, things change."

Mother and daughter traded stares in silence.

"I should go …" Everett broke the silence after a long and uncomfortably awkward moment.

"You don't need to go, Everett. Harmony is going back to her room to study for—"

"Shouldn't you be proud of me that I'm not dumb enough to waste my effort on idiotic—"

"School isn't stupid, Harmony. Your grades are important and they have slipped. *Significantly.*"

"Sorry. Let me phrase: *School is irrelevant to my future.*"

"You do realize that opting out of college isn't something you can't just take back?"

"That's your argument?" Harmony laughed. "Of course I can take it back. I could go to ACC, or literally any community college in the country. I could get my general credits, then enroll in a 'real college' as a junior, when it'll be way easier to get in. And without wasting my money."

"Oh, it's your money now?" Klair raised her eyebrows. "You're actually planning to pay your way for once?"

Harmony flushed scarlet with anger. Or humiliation?

Everett wished he was anywhere else in the world.

"Your father and I expect more from you. This is your senior year."

"You never even give me credit when I'm trying my best."

"What do you think your father would say if he knew about my little chat with your guidance counselor today?"

"I don't know." Then, with what sounded to Everett like definite fear in her voice, Harmony added, "Are you going to tell him?"

"If this isn't turned around by midterms, then yes, absolutely."

He didn't have any right to offer an opinion. But Klair had told him to stay and witness this argument. Because she expected him to stand in for his brother? Or because she thought Harmony would back down in front of company?

He decided that Klair wouldn't have asked him to stay

if she didn't want his perspective. "If I were Evan, I'd want to know that my daughter was struggling."

"You know what, Rhett? I was wrong." Klair shook her head. "You should go."

"Yeah, Rhett. Stay out of it." Harmony spun around and marched toward the stairs, using Everett as an excuse to flee the scene.

Klair gave Everett another dirty look, then took off after her daughter.

And then he was all alone, feeling like an asshole, still holding his basket of laundry.

"My name is *Everett*," he muttered under his breath.

Then he explored until he found the washer and dryer, in a tidy little room just behind the kitchen. What had he been thinking? Why was it impossible for him to go a day without ruining something?

Probably because he was always sticking his nose where it didn't belong.

As he loaded his laundry into the washer, he thought about how he'd ruined things with Clara, and now he was in danger of ruining things with Jimi. Everett hated when she said it, but he *was* a fuckup.

Did he even deserve to be a father?

He stood in the small laundry room listening to the washer hum for a minute or so before finally turning around and leaving with a long sigh.

He definitely wouldn't be invited to family dinner tonight. His guest house fridge was now mostly empty, but he didn't feel right rifling through the family fridge inside.

So he left the house and went for a stroll, through the neighborhood and onto Bee Cave, then down a gently sloping hill toward a pair of shopping centers nestled at the bottom, one on either side of the street. The one to his left contained a small restaurant called Norma's, where Everett ordered himself a burger and onion rings.

He ate his dinner at a table for one, feeling pleased with his progress today, but dreading tomorrow.

Because it was time to have a difficult talk with his brother.

Chapter Twenty-Six

EVERETT surprised himself by waking up before the alarm went off. But he couldn't drift back to sleep, because thoughts of his impending financial doom were creeping in. So he showered and dressed, intending to go for a walk before he headed to Señor Sushi for another day of training with real customers.

But as he reached for the knob of the guest house's front door, someone knocked. His first thought was that Klair had come to kick him out.

But when he opened the door, he saw a grinning Evan holding two travel mugs.

"Morning. You finish your morning jerk session yet?"

Everett froze, not sure how he should answer.

"I'm just kidding. Shit." Evan laughed and shoved his brother, playfully pushing his way inside while leaving the door ajar behind him. "Want a ride in?"

"I would love that."

"How long before you're ready to jet?"

"I was just heading out."

Evan was in an excellent mood, but not exactly chatty

as he sipped his coffee and drove. But the travel mugs were filled with some of the best coffee Everett had ever tasted, and he thought of Lena's repeated suggestions that he offer a selection of high-end beans instead of competing with all the fancy, sweet drinks served by the chains.

Everett took out his phone to check his supplier's website, but got distracted by a text from his bank that he'd missed last night. He was overdrawn. One of his recurring payments must have cleared. And he couldn't count on anything coming in from the café; without him around, Java Joe's probably wasn't even bringing in enough to cover Lena's wages. No doubt his business credit line was close to maxed. And when it hit the limit, Lena would close shop over working for a week or two without pay.

And all he had left was a personal credit card that was closing in on its max.

He shouldn't have eaten at Norma's last night. Spending that much on a meal when there was food in the house had been a dumb thing to do.

He had no other choice. He was going to have to ask Evan to either spot him some money, or pay him to work in the restaurant.

"You know what?" Everett wasn't sure where his *You know what?* was going to lead, but he had to kick the conversation into motion.

"Can you hold that thought until we get to the restaurant?" Evan answered while staring straight ahead. "I'm right in the middle of sorting a few things in my head and don't want to lose track."

"Of course!" Everett replied like an overly enthusiastic idiot.

He looked back at his phone, wishing that he'd waited for a better time. Now Evan was probably thinking that he didn't know how to be comfortable with silence, exactly like Clara was always accusing him of.

Everett checked his email and saw the custody paperwork. The sight put a tickle of sweat on each of his temples. He swallowed as the reality sank in. His weekends with Jimi were once the best thing in his life, and he hadn't appreciated them nearly as much as he should have. Now his existence would feel that much more hollow.

"You did great yesterday," Evan said as he pulled into the parking lot and killed the engine. "Let's do that again today." He clapped his brother on the shoulder and got out of the car.

Everett needed another couple of moments in his seat, feeling stupidly, embarrassingly emotional.

How could he ask for anything after that?

In the kitchen, he donned his apron, prepped his station, then washed up and got started. Morris and Bernardo weren't in yet. Everything happened in an elegant silence, only the clinking and clanking of utensils amid the shuffling of rubber soles against vinyl flooring and the occasional *THWAP* of ingredients plopping onto the counter. It was the closest Everett had ever gotten to meditation.

"You're doing great," Evan said out of nowhere.

Everett had never felt so hopeful. But at the same time, Evan's appreciation made it even harder to ask for the money. A request right now felt like ingratitude.

Morris strutted in, winked at Everett, and started arranging his station.

Opportunity lost.

That was probably for the best. Dropping a conversational bomb like *there's something we need to talk about* right before the start of their day would have surely been a mistake.

Bernardo joined them, and they moved as a unit, preparing the kitchen for service. Señor Sushi was spotless, thanks to The Law According to Evan Shepherd: *Any employee with a spare moment should be using it to clean.* The taste of a dish was subjective, but no one had ever complained about Evan's restaurant being dirty, and no one ever would.

The lunch rush became the dinner rush. It was heads down for hours after that, working next to Morris who kept his hands moving and his station mate entertained with a series of *bitches* that seemed to constantly escalate in the complexity of his usage. Bernardo offered Everett several compliments throughout the day, all of them in passing and one he would remember forever.

Now I see that you are his brother.

They left the restaurant late, after Evan prepared them a quick bite to eat, then drove home in a pristine silence that Everett found impossible to shatter. And honestly, as painful as it was to keep delaying the conversation, maybe it was for the best. Because after thinking more about the remodel his landlord would require, Everett had realized it would be so much smarter to ask Evan for an investment. Evan would rather be a partner in his business than a brother loaning his loser twin money out of pity.

Evan swung into his driveway with a sigh. "Another great day, my man."

"Yeah ... my favorite so far." *Still not the time. Don't ruin it.*

"I. Am. Beat."

"I'm glad to hear you say it." Everett laughed. "I feel like a little bitch, and you did so much more than me."

"You did plenty. And you're clearly working with Morris too much.

Everett laughed again.

"You want a glass of wine before bed?" Evan nodded toward his front door. "It's good for the heart."

"Is the same true for whiskey?"

"No."

"Then wine sounds great," Everett said.

Evan chuckled and opened his car door.

Even so obviously exhausted, this was the loosest toward him that Everett had felt so far. How better to invite Evan to back Java Joe's than over a glass of wine?

He followed Evan into the kitchen where Klair leaned against the island, her entire body tilted as she swirled a goblet of red wine in what looked like a pantomime of *Wife waiting impatiently for husband.*

So much for the perfect time to ask.

"What is it?" Evan was by her side immediately.

"What do you think it is?"

"I've had a long day. Can you please just tell me?"

Once again, he found himself trapped in a conflict that wasn't his. It felt rude to stay, and rude to walk out without being excused.

"Our son has been suspended from school. For a week. And do you know *why*?"

Evan sighed. "For fighting?"

"For fighting," Klair confirmed with a scowl.

"So you would like for me to talk—"

"Damn right I want you to talk to him." Then she drained her goblet and left the kitchen.

Evan turned to Everett. "I don't understand what's happening with Jazz lately, or how to talk to him about whatever it is."

Everett wanted to help, but most of his interventions thus far had backfired.

Tentatively, he said, "Jazz and I were talking about his situation just a few days ago."

"Oh yeah?" Evan asked, lit by a happy kind of surprise.

"Yeah." This already felt great. "Without breaking any uncle-nephew confidentiality, I feel comfortable telling you that Jazz doesn't want to fight. The other kids are bullying him."

Evan exhaled, a mighty gust that seemed like it had probably been trapped in his soul for months. "Thank you. It's been so hard to connect with him lately."

"You're doing your best," Everett assured him.

"But I'm not doing enough." Evan shook his head. "I'm always talking about balancing the restaurants. Shit, man. I need to think about balancing my family."

That is what Klair keeps telling you.

"I'm going to fix everything. Once Tequila launches, the Shepherds will return to a new normal, and our lives will be better than ever."

"That sounds great."

"But right now I need to find a new normal with Jazz." Evan nodded toward the stairs. "Wish me luck."

"Good luck," Everett said.

He really could've used that glass of wine.

Chapter Twenty-Seven

EVERETT WAS STILL RADIATING an ugly heat from witnessing the exchange between Evan and Klair.

He absorbed it all in the moment because he had no other choice. But now, still standing in their kitchen a full minute later, he realized how much their little argument had actually shaken him. Her eyes were … *intense*. Thinking about it now, Everett wondered if that expression had been bred more from hurt or from anger.

He ran a hand through his hair, wondering what he should do. Waiting around for Evan was surely a mistake. The kids had probably been in bed for a while. And he *really* didn't want Klair coming back into the kitchen while he was still there. Not while her eyes looked like that.

He should get out of here and back to the guest house.

But Klair walked in before he could leave, her eyes red and swollen from crying.

She picked up her empty goblet. But instead of walking to the sink, she went to the wine rack.

"Red or white?" She looked at Everett expectantly.

He didn't want either, if it meant getting entangled

with a tipsy Klair. He should go to bed and give Evan some space to talk things through with her. But maybe he could help his brother out. Calm her down by having a drink with her.

Besides, impending financial doom was not the most restful situation to be in. He would sleep better if he had a glass or two in him.

"Whatever you're having."

She grabbed a bottle and a second glass, and poured far too much wine for both of them. Hopefully Evan would be done talking with Jazz before they'd drunk a quarter of it.

"I wanted to apologize for yesterday," he said, accepting the overfull glass she handed him.

"*Shh*," she said.

Everett didn't know what that meant. Was he not supposed to say anything about yesterday, or anything at all? He took a sip to kill some time, knowing he needed to get out of the kitchen. Whatever this was, it wasn't good.

"I should never have inserted myself into the—"

"I said *shh*." She pointed to his glass with what was left of hers. "Drink."

"I'm not really—"

"You can leave when you're finished."

So he drank, not too fast, but more than a casual sip, and definitely more than he wanted. His glass was still half-full, or perhaps in this situation half-empty was more like it.

"What has it been like, working at the restaurant?" she asked, refilling her already-empty glass.

"Are you sure—"

"Am I sure what, Rhett?" She glared at him, daring him with her eyes.

"That you want to know what it's been like working at the restaurant," he replied like a coward.

"Why wouldn't I want to know that?"

"Because isn't that part of the problem here?" What in the hell was he saying? "That Evan is always talking about work?"

"Evan *is* always talking about work," she agreed, her words more slurred than before. "Do you always talk about work, Rhett? Is that why you're divorced?"

"That was part of it, yes." So. Uncomfortable. "But watching Evan work, it's inspiring how much your husband puts in. He's giving me great ideas that I can't wait to try once I'm back home."

"And when will that be, Rhett? How much longer will you be living right outside our house?" Despite her slurred words, Klair's voice was so perfectly neutral that Everett had no idea if she was asking him to stay, or telling him to leave.

"I'll be going home as soon as Tequila Mockingbird opens."

"Listen to you: *Tequila Mockingbird.*" She laughed. "Just like you're one of the family."

Words he longed to hear, but without the sarcasm.

Everett glanced down at his half-full glass, then drank the rest of his wine in several large gulps.

"Whoa there, tiger," said Klair.

"I was thirsty," he lied.

"No you weren't," she slurred. "You want to get away from me." A sideways smile. "Isn't that right, Rhett?"

"I do think it's time to go."

"You're uncomfortable because you care."

That is not at all why I'm uncomfortable.

"You're uncomfortable because you know that Evan *doesn't* care about us. At least not like he used to." Her words were coming more frantically. "You know because you're new to the situation. You can see how he is now instead of how he used to be." She stopped, just long enough to show Everett the depths of her sorrow. "He hasn't cared for a long time, Rhett. Not about us. Not like he cares about his stupid restaurant." Then she corrected herself. "*Restaurants.*"

"That's not true, Klair."

"What do you know?" Now it looked like she wanted to spit on him.

"As we were coming home, Evan said that he was always talking about balancing the two restaurants, but that he really needed to think about balancing his family."

"My husband is great at thinking. And doing, assuming the doing involves his career."

"It won't be much longer until the restaurant is open, and—"

"So: *restaurant first.*"

"He really is trying hard." And honestly, it felt like Klair was refusing to see Evan's side of things. "I know he wants to fix what's breaking, or broken, and that's one of the reasons I'm still here. Because I know that once the restaurant is open, Evan will be family first. I want to help make that happen."

"Listen to you." Klair set her glass on the counter. "Not only are you working your ass off in your brother's restaurant, you're also working overtime to save his marriage."

"I'm just doing what he would do for me."

"We both know that's not true," Klair said with a fragile shake of her head.

And then her lips were on his.

He pushed her away. "This can't happen."

"You know you've thought about it." She tried again.

And again he pushed her away. "Evan would be furious with me."

"So that's the only reason." Klair made eyes at him. "What if I asked his permission ... what would you say then, Rhett?"

"Nothing. I wouldn't say anything."

Everett turned to leave, but she darted in front of him.

"I bet you would say *something*."

Then she jumped into his arms and pressed her lips to his again.

Everett pushed her away ... just as Evan entered the kitchen with a roar.

"WHAT THE HELL IS GOING ON HERE?"

"I was trying to remember what it was like when you used to want me," Klair said.

"I wasn't doing anything ..." Everett raised his hands. "Not to drag out the old cliché *this isn't what it looks like*, but from my side, man, it really *really* isn't."

"Please do just shut up, Rhett," Klair suggested.

Evan glared at her.

"What the hell were *you* thinking?"

"I should go."

"Really?" Evan reeled toward his brother. "You don't want to finish what you started?"

"He didn't start anything," Klair said.

"The only thing you could have possibly seen me doing is pushing her away."

"Jesus Christ, Rhett."

Was Klair insulted that he'd rejected her, or disgusted that he seemed to care more about Evan's feelings than hers?

"Maybe we can talk about this tomorrow." When everyone was sober. Because the wine was hitting him all at once, and as intoxication mingled with his adrenaline rush, the wave of dizziness just about knocked Everett off his feet.

"He won't talk to me if you leave, Rhett. Not about this. He'll bitch at me for drinking and he'll be pissed at me for weeks about my trying to kiss you. But he won't ever talk about the real problem."

Evan seemed paralyzed. Everett could relate. That was always how he felt when Clara started in on him.

Klair continued. "Every time you've had a chance to put your family ahead of the restaurant, things went the other way around instead. You live in this dreamland where Harmony and Jazz are all grown up. Where they don't need us anymore and you can be gone all day and night, every day of the week if that's what it takes. You act like I don't need you. Like I don't miss you. Like I don't have feelings or wants … or goals that have nothing to do with yours!"

It was like déjà vu, the same fight he'd had with Clara the day before she announced her desire to get a divorce.

Evan waited for Klair to take another breath before he responded. "I hear everything you're saying, and you're right, I've been putting my career in front of you guys. And I can see how that's affecting Jazz and Harmony. How it's affecting us. We're not the team we used to be, and I know that's all my fault."

"*But*," she sneered. "Go ahead and say it, because there's always a *but*."

"Everything will change once the new restaurant is open. We're in the final stretch."

That was the same thing he'd told Clara. *Everything will change once I get the foot traffic up. We're in the final stretch.* That had been his mistake, thinking it was all about the restaurant, when it had really been all about Clara's feelings. If he'd made her happiness a condition of the restaurant's success, instead of making the restaurant's success a condition of her happiness, they might still be together.

And now he had to stand by and watch his brother make the same mistake.

"We've been in the final stretch for months, Evan. And you've been racing down every twist and turn of that final stretch going thirty miles over the speed limit, while I'm sitting shotgun without a seatbelt!"

"I under—"

"I DON'T THINK YOU DO!"

"You're both right, and you're both wrong," Everett tried.

But that was the wrong thing to do.

They turned toward him in unison, angrier at him than they were with each other.

"I'm just—"

"You're just nothing," Evan cut him off. "Actually, never mind. You are *just something*. You're just leaving. Get the hell out of here."

"I—"

"*Now.*" Evan's eyes were harder than Everett had ever seen them. "I don't need a twin, especially one like you. No need for an adios in the morning."

His eyes bored into Everett's. The meaning in his gaze couldn't be clearer.

You've done enough damage here.

Chapter Twenty-Eight

EVERETT COULDN'T SLEEP. He'd packed everything, straightened up the guest house, done his best to leave things as he'd found them. Maybe it was for the best. If he drove all night, he could get to Clara's house in time to take Jimi, leaving her free to catch that flight to Nashville in pursuit of her dream. Maybe she'd even reconsidering the custody thing, if she saw how serious he was about being there for their son. Although it was probably best not to count on that.

Maybe he could get a job in Nashville while he rebuilt his credit and supported Jimi through the next phases of his life.

But he couldn't leave without apologizing to Evan. Whether Evan wanted an apology or not.

So he stayed awake through the night, not wanting to miss his chance.

Mercifully, the back door to the main house was unlocked when he tried it. And the kitchen was rich with the aroma of coffee.

But when he went to the window, he saw that the black Tesla was gone from the driveway, and whispered a string of curses.

He couldn't just tuck his tail between his legs and run home. Not until he'd made things right.

He kept expecting to see Klair or Harmony or Jazz appear out of nowhere, and demand to know what the exiled stranger was doing on their property. Inside their house. Uninvited yet still in their lives.

He hurried back to the guest house for his wallet and keys. Then he hit the road.

Evan was almost for sure at Señor's right now, banging his head against the wall while frantically trying to come up with a plan to replace the brother who had betrayed him. Or would he be at Tequila, mourning the financial hit he'd take by delaying the opening until Gabriel returned?

He was sure that the plan had been for another practice run with live customers, so it had to be Señor.

It was easy to imagine the scene from Evan's perspective, walking in and seeing Klair in his brother's arms. Not that she was *in his arms* so much as *pushing herself into them.* Everett would never hit on her. Not in a million years.

But Evan would have to see that.

Except ... Everett *had* been attracted to her. He and Evan had so much in common, it made absolute sense that they would have the same or similar taste in women.

Had he encouraged Klair in some way without even realizing it? The thought that he might be at least partially responsible for the destruction of his brother's marriage was unbearable. Because if successful, disciplined Evan couldn't help making the same mistakes Everett had, then Everett was doomed. He was never going to sort things out with Clara, or get his life together.

Shame writhed inside him. Because there was no denying that a part of him fumed with jealousy. Evan's marriage could be saved. Everett would give anything to still have that chance with Clara.

He parked next to his brother's black Tesla, grateful that he'd guessed right.

He slammed the Mustang door, then ran across the lot and right into the kitchen. The bustle sounded well ahead of schedule. Bodies scurrying about amid of blitzkrieg of the chef's barked commands.

Evan glanced over, saw Everett, then looked right through him, walking by like his brother didn't even exist.

"I just need a minute, then I'm out of here. Back to California. You'll never have to hear from me again if you don't want to. I promise."

But he couldn't even get Evan to acknowledge his existence. A conversation was clearly out of the question.

"I don't mean to be a bitch or nothing, but you should probably get out of here," Morris suggested with a cool whisper once he managed to get Everett alone, after Evan stormed into the walk-in. "You kissed his woman."

Morris was probably right, but he couldn't give up.

As Everett headed for the walk-in, Bernardo took him by the arm and led him out of the kitchen. "You have to go home."

"I can't go anywhere until—"

"Go home, Rhett." Bernardo shook his head. "If you stick around after you have been asked to go, repeatedly and explicitly, you are only doing more damage to your relationship."

"I can't drive all the way back to California without—"

"Then don't," Bernardo cut him off, clearly needing to get back inside. "Go to your guest house. Wait for Chef there. Give him some space and I am sure that everything will work out eventually. There's nothing more you can do here. Do you understand?"

Everett did understand. He just hated the truth.

Chapter Twenty-Nine

AFTER MORE THAN an hour of pacing the guest house, Everett could no longer stand it.

He grabbed his phone, and dialed Derek.

Three rings, then Derek said, "Yo! I know you must still be in a different time zone if your ass is calling me this early. Or you're dying. Are you dying, Everett?"

"No ... I'm not dying ... not literally, anyway." Only after the words were all out did he realize how close to crying he was.

Derek sobered immediately. "What do you need, man? Just tell me what we can do."

Everett did his best to deliver the *Reader's Digest* version to Derek, even the most humiliating parts that he would usually leave out, ending with the request he'd initially intended for Evan. "So I need enough money to pay for the Mustang when I drop it off, cover whatever I need to pay the mechanic in El Paso, then get the rest of the way home with gas and food and whatever. Can you please help me out?"

Derek sighed. "If I send you extra, will you promise to

leave that piece of shit in El Paso and fly home? Devon and I can help you find a new piece of shit when you're back."

"Thanks man. I really appreciate it."

"I know you do," Derek said.

They hung up and Everett took one last look around the guest house before leaving it all behind forever.

He had driven to Austin with a dream. But he had ruined that fantasy by paying more attention to the things his new family could do for him, instead of considering all the ways he could make himself essential to his new family.

Maybe things were actually better this way. He had inserted himself into Evan's world, wrongly assuming that his brother had an Everett-shaped hole just waiting to be filled. Though far from perfect, Evan's life was still a dream come true for Everett.

What had he been thinking? Driving from California to Austin without any warning, assuming he would be welcomed with open arms.

Hey, you don't know me from Adam, but we do share DNA, so I was figuring that maybe we could be buddies? BFFs, even. How about I sweeten the deal with some video games? Don't I look trust-worthy in my new clothes? I got them at Redford Creek, because that's where Texas gets dressed!

He was such a moron sometimes.

He took out his phone and checked to see if the money from Derek's transfer had cleared his account. But nope, his balance still showed the same disaster, which meant he wouldn't be going anywhere quite yet.

He should have listened to his best friends when they were trying to give him good advice. He could have called Evan first, or friended him on LiveLyfe. Tried to nurture an actual relationship instead of acting as if the deep connection he'd been longing for his entire life already existed.

He had been living a loser's life in California. Finding his twin brother was never going to change that. He'd ruined his own marriage and was struggling in his relationship with his son. Because he didn't appreciate them until he lost them.

And the biggest revelation of all: *Evan and I are the same, but not how I thought.*

Evan's mistakes were the spitting image of his own.

He pulled out his phone and recorded a short video for his son.

"Hey there, Jimi ..." Everett was Dad, making his goofiest face. "I just wanted to tell you how much I've been missing you! Our weekends mean everything to me, little man. And I *hate* that I've missed a few. I'm in Austin right now — that's in Texas, which is even bigger than California, but not bigger than Alaska." Everett found himself smiling, thinking about how much Jimi always enjoyed little factoids like that. "I'm here because I found out that I have a twin brother! That's right, just like Devon and Derek. I'll be home soon, but I wanted to say *hi* and let you know that you're the most important thing in the world to me."

Everett pressed *End*, a half-second before the first tear fell, then sent it in a text to Clara:

Can you please show this to Jimi for me? Tell him I love him and that I'll be home soon. I'm really sorry about our last couple of arguments. I can and will do better.

Whether or not he could convince Clara to drop her petition for sole custody, he would move to Nashville, or anywhere else that she decided to take his son.

He just needed some money.

He checked his balance again.

The funds were finally available.

He would try one more time to make things right with Evan.

Then he would spend the rest of his life making sure Jimi had the father he deserved.

EVERETT ARRIVED AT SEÑOR SUSHI, surprised to find it closed — due to a family emergency, according to the note on the door. Another guilty twinge, because that's how Evan would remember him, as a family emergency that had to be dealt with.

Everett kept the music loud on his way to Tequila Mockingbird.

He needed to be flooded with noise. Otherwise his brain kept trying to play tricks on him, insisting that he was making another big mistake, even though he knew in his soul that this couldn't be more right. It was still difficult, keeping his foot on the gas while knowing he was not welcome. He could picture Evan's scowl, and feel his scorn even without being near him.

But he couldn't let that detour him.

No matter what happened — and Everett was fully prepared for a total catastrophe — he had to try. He was willing to demean himself, humiliate himself, work himself to the marrow. Whatever it took — anything to ensure that Tequila's opening not only went off without a hitch, but that it left Evan with enough runway to go home in peace and repair the recent tears in his family life.

He parked the Mustang, across the lot from that shiny black Tesla, then ran toward the entrance.

He heard loud voices inside, the clanging of pots and pans, the scurrying of bodies and the squeaking of feet. But none of it in concert with anything else. For once, the tune of Evan's typically orderly world sounded discordant. He entered the kitchen and witnessed a sight that was as new to him as the cacophony — Evan in mid-meltdown, railing on his station chiefs.

Morris saw him first, and shook his head violently, trying to warn Everett away. But naturally, Evan caught the movement and whirled around, stopping mid-rant.

Then huffed right by his twin brother without so much as a word.

"You gotta get outta here, bitch," Morris said in a growling whisper. "Like *now*."

"I know. But—"

"I mean it, bitch." Morris shook his head fast, looking anxious, like an addict desperate to score. "This isn't a rampage, it's a war path. He'll be adding a Dumbass Bitch Brain Relleno to the menu if you're here when he comes back. I'm serious."

"What's wrong?"

"Everything, bitch."

"Can you be more specific?"

Morris threw his hands in the air and muttered under his breath. "You've gotta be kidding me."

The kitchen doors swung open again. Bernardo, walking right toward them. Softly to Everett he said, "Please, it is better for everyone if you go."

"That's what I keep telling him!" Morris exclaimed.

"I promise to leave as soon as someone tells me why he's so upset. This isn't just about me."

Bernardo sighed, looking into Everett's eyes and surely seeing that a short explanation was the most expedient way of getting him out of there. "Your brother made a big mistake yesterday."

"Chef done fucked up." Morris shook his head.

"He was ... upset. He messed up the opening order."

Still shaking his head: "Our ingredients and our menu don't match."

Bernardo looked grave. "The menu Chef has been working on for months."

"The one we've been practicing up in this bitch since whenever," Morris added.

There must be something more to it, because this sounded like a solvable problem. "But you do have ingredients, right? Can't you just tweak the menu?"

"This isn't about using coconut milk if you run out of almond milk, or putting a *Sold Out!* sign on the decaf when you didn't order enough. I am sorry to say it, Rhett," Bernardo shook his head, "but your experience doesn't apply here."

Ouch.

"Just … explain it to me. *Please.* Why can't—"

"Eggs and oaths are easily broken," Bernardo muttered, turning away from Everett and heading back to the kitchen.

"Look, bitch, I gotta jet, I don't need Bernardo pissed at me, too. Chef's gonna wanna grate my scrote for even talking to you, so I'mma microwave this explanation. Like, we need an entirely different menu. And Evan already told people what to expect."

"So, say it's a special opening day menu?"

"Restaurant suicide." Morris dragged a finger across his neck. "Journalists, critics, self-important bloggers, every bitch in the city with an opinion to share. This is bigger than the typical opening for sure, but nice as it is to be at the top, the fall from up high is one hell of a bitch."

"Can't we just go shopping to get some new ingredients? I know it will cost more to get what we need at Central Market or wherever, but—"

"Just stop." Morris shook his head, holding a hand

palm out to stop Everett from saying anything else. "I don't mean to be a bitch, but we barely know each other. We're not friends enough for me to risk losing my job. You need to go. Okay?"

"What if I really can help? Please, Morris …" Then again, with every ounce of emotion he had. "*Please*. One minute. That's it. You give me one more minute and not only will I be out of here if I can't figure out a way to help, but I swear on my son's life that you'll never see me again."

"Well shit, bitch. Sixty seconds, starting now."

"Fast as you can, tell me why we can't get what we need at the grocery store."

"*Way* too expensive. And we're talking specialty peppers from all over Texas and Mexico. Mirasols, arbols, chilhuacle rojos. And some you probably have heard of, like cascabels and guajillos. Special-order shit that Chef was sure he had special ordered. But what he actually ordered? Boxes and boxes and *boxes* of plain old red bell peppers."

"He can't make a single one of the regional dishes he had planned without peppers from that region. Well, he can, but they won't taste authentic. They're going to taste like an American made th— why are you looking at me like that?"

"Has it been a minute?"

"I guess?" Morris was still looking at him, perplexed. "You got a plan?"

Everett grinned. "You bet I do, bitch."

Chapter Thirty

EVERETT PULLED up to Tequila Mockingbird, then sat for a moment after he'd killed the engine. It was a relief to see Evan's Tesla parked alongside two cars that he assumed belonged to Morris and Bernardo. Everyone was still here. So they hadn't given up yet.

Did he really want to do this? It was a huge risk, and if it didn't go well, it might destroy any remaining chance of repairing his relationship with Evan. If there had been any kind of twin bond between them, Everett's constant butting in had destroyed it. Or maybe the Ds were right, and what looked like a magical bond from the outside was the result of being raised together.

If that was the case, Everett's quest to experience that closeness had been doomed from the start.

But none of that mattered now, because this wasn't about the twin bond. It was about apologizing for the damage he'd done by trying to shove his way into Evan's life, and offering up a parting gift before returning to his own life in California.

He hurried to the front door, which he discovered was

unlocked — probably from when Evan had thrown him out this morning — and peeked inside. The dining area was empty, although there should have been a couple members of the waitstaff setting up for tomorrow.

Evan and the others were probably holed up in the kitchen, scrambling to assemble a new menu from scratch. Or frantically calling suppliers, hoping to find enough of the ingredients they needed to execute on the original menu.

So he unpacked the pots and baking pans a few at a time, quietly carrying them inside and placing them on an empty table in a quiet corner of the dining room. Hopefully Klair wouldn't be too angry when she came home and found his note, promising to bring them back and wash them all this evening.

Each one contained a dish based on one of his mother's best recipes, combining the ingredients they'd been practicing with all week and the red bell peppers Evan had accidentally ordered. Plus a few things they could easily get from Central Market.

Tri-tip street tacos with caramelized onions and red peppers, topped with arugula, then drizzled with cilantro-lime crema and roasted tomatillo salsa.

Shrimp fajitas redolent with garlic and cumin, grilled with red peppers, tomatoes, onions and sliced jalapenos, and garnished with cilantro sour cream and crumbled Oaxacan cheese.

Halibut marinated in Mom's chile-lime sauce, then seared and served with a generous dollop of roasted red pepper relish and a side of chevre.

Chicken enchiladas topped with roasted red pepper sauce with a hint of warmth from the single habanero he'd thrown in, and finished with crema, guacamole, and corn salsa.

And his favorite, a simple tilapia stew with a tomato and roasted red pepper base, brightened with a splash of lemon juice, and spiced with chipotle, garlic and Mexican oregano, whose citrusy undertones beat the flavor of the Italian variety any day.

He'd done his best to marry the Tex-Mex approach with the Baja flavor palate that his mother had loved so much. It was nothing like the dishes Evan had planned to make, but if they made the soup base and the sauces today, preparing dishes they hadn't rehearsed would be simpler. Enchiladas were still enchiladas, and halibut seared the same no matter what it was marinated in.

He was summoning the courage to walk back to the kitchen when Morris emerged into the dining room, then stopped as he caught sight of Everett.

"Bitch, do you not underst—" Morris blinked and shook his head like someone had just slapped him. "What the fuck am I smelling?"

Evan marched in and swore as soon as he saw Everett, stopping so abruptly that Bernardo, who followed behind, almost ran into him.

Evan glared at Everett and jammed his finger at the door.

"Hear me out," Everett said. "And then, I promise, you'll never see me again."

Morris muttered something about bitches with balls under his breath.

Bernardo stared at the food-laden table like he was dying to try it, if only it wouldn't cost him his job.

Evan pointed at the door again.

Everett took the lid off the tilapia stew. His brother's nostrils flared in response — trying to deconstruct the scent into flavors. He probably couldn't help it.

"If you don't want my help, I understand," Everett said

as he removed the covers on the rest of the dishes. "But I ruined everything by showing up unannounced, and I can't leave without trying to fix things one more time. So I'm asking you to taste these dishes based on my mother's recipes, all of which are built around the ingredients you actually have in the kitchen. If you love them, you're free to use them or modify them for tomorrow's opening. If you decide they're not good enough, then at least you won't be hungry while you're coming up with another plan."

Evan didn't move a muscle.

But Morris approached the table and picked up a tri-tip taco, taking a giant bite. As he chewed, he made a surprised face — and after he swallowed, he turned to Bernardo and Evan. "Dibs on taking these home."

Bernardo disappeared into the back, then reappeared with a stack of plates, bowls and silverware, and thrust them into Everett's hands. "Serve us."

Everett quickly plated out a small portion of each dish and set a spot for the three chefs at the next table, followed by a bowl of the fish stew, and finally, a complete set of silverware.

Morris sat and immediately started digging in, making moaning noises around a mouthful of shrimp fajitas. Bernardo smacked the back of his head before taking his own seat in a more dignified way.

Evan continued to glare at Everett.

"Think of it as celebrating my departure," Everett suggested.

Evan shook his head, then sat and began to taste the food — starting with the stew. Everett couldn't help holding his breath. Not because he wasn't sure the soup was good — it was — but because if Evan hated it, it would almost be like Evan hating Everett's mother. Irrational, but that's how much he missed her. She'd made that stew for him when he was sick, when he was recovering from his brothers' beatings, and even when he was playing sick because school had become so unbearable, another day of it made his stomach hurt.

That stew, and everything she cooked for him, was how Mom had showed her love.

And if he made it for himself now that she was gone, that would be like sending flowers to himself on Valentine's Day: not an expression of love at all, but a desperate attempt to pretend that someone loved him, when deep down, he knew that no one was ever going to love him again like his mother had.

But cooking it for Evan, who he was just starting to love, that felt right. Even if Everett never saw his brother again, passing that affection on to him was the best possible thing he could do with his mother's old recipes. That was what they were for, not to be hoarded, but to be shared with the people he loved.

But Evan paused after he swallowed the first spoonful of stew, his face void of expression. Then he methodically tried each item on his plate while staring ahead.

After taking one bite of everything, he finally stood from the table and walked back to the kitchen, without looking back.

Everett felt a stabbing pain in his chest, and he bit the inside of his cheek to keep from crying.

Evan had given him a chance, and that had to be good enough.

"Wow, bitches …" Morris shook his head, breaking the silence and taking a sliver of tension with it. "These camarónes are on fire."

"I am sorry that did not go better," Bernardo said to Everett, whose throat was too tight for the manufacture of words.

"No shit. Now that he's gone, I don't mind saying that Chef is being kind of an asshole." Morris nodded at the pan of enchiladas. "You mind? You're not taking that back home, right?"

Back home.

It hurt so much already.

The guest house wasn't home, and never had been, but somehow California didn't feel like home anymore, either. Everett had come to Austin believing that his life was going to change, but not like this. He'd thought he was going to be more connected now that he had a twin brother, not disconnected from everything.

He was on the verge of crying again, but Bernardo began to grill him. *Did he put lemon or lime juice in the relish? Where was the hint of smoke in enchilada sauce coming from? What was the tomato-to-pepper ratio in the stew base?*

Everett was grateful to Bernardo for pulling him back from his emotional cliff by asking a battery of technical questions. As he answered, he glanced at the hallway leading to the kitchen, but apparently Evan wanted nothing to do with his brother.

"Our rush order is only a day behind," Bernardo said to Morris. "We could run with the regular menu starting the day after tomorrow. This could work."

"Damn right it could work!" Morris added before stuffing another shrimp into his mouth and chewing with gusto.

Everett pulled a stack of index cards from his back pocket and dropped them onto the table. "I wrote it all down. If you make the sauces and the soup base today, and get everything marinating, tomorrow will be a lot like the menu we've been practicing for. I'd offer to stay and help, but I doubt Evan will want that."

"Don't take it personal," Morris said around another full mouth. "Chef's just like that."

"I believe that someday your brother will be able to see the man you are, but that's probably not happening today," Bernardo added. "You know he's going to tweak the dishes, even though they're amazing, right?"

Of course Evan would make the recipes his own; how could he not? The only thing that mattered was that his brother's restaurant — and his marriage — might be saved.

"It was really great meeting and working with both of you." Everett gave them each an appreciative nod. "I learned a lot, and had fun. Thanks for everything."

"Me three." Morris clapped him on the shoulder. "This right here is some shit."

"Safe journey," Bernardo said.

"Tell him I hope this place is a huge success," Everett said.

He trudged out to the parking lot, taking one long look at Tequila Mockingbird and imagining the place packed with happy customers, raving about Evan's cooking.

Or maybe they would complain that the food was not at all what Evan had promised in the months leading up to the opening.

Either way, there was nothing more Everett could do to help.

But with luck, Evan would keep his promise to Klair and find a way to devote more time to his family.

Now it was time to go home and do right by Jimi and Clara.

Everett turned the engine, tapped on the gas, and immediately slammed on the brakes.

Bernardo was running out of the restaurant, wildly waving his arms overhead.

He put the Mustang in park, rolled down the window, then waited for Bernardo to come lumbering over.

"What's wrong?" Everett asked when he got there. "What did I do?"

"You didn't do anything wrong." Bernardo laughed. "Chef's going with your recipes, and I convinced him that we still can't handle the opening without another station chef. Would you like to work opening day?"

"Does Chef want me to?"

"Beggars can't be choosers," Bernardo warned. "Are you going to help us out or not?"

Everett grinned. "I'd be honored."

Chapter Thirty-One

EVERETT MIGHT HAVE SAID that the restaurant was a madhouse, if the kitchen wasn't so orderly. Evan was a demon on the main grill, barking his needs without ever turning around to look at whoever had jumped to carry out his command. But the sauces were ready to go, the meat was well-marinated, and mountains of vegetables had been chopped. Everett stayed on his station and moved each item down to Morris as quickly as he could without sacrificing the perfection that Evan demanded from all of them.

The hardest part was staying synchronized with the other three men, but it got easier as he willed himself to relax and focus on the food. Not on Evan, and how mad he still was at Everett. Not on how Morris and Bernardo constantly slung teasing insults at each other as they worked. And not on how he'd be leaving tomorrow, because he still hadn't earned the right to be here.

He focused on the staccato rhythm of Bernardo's knife instead, the sizzle of halibut and shrimp on the grill, and the clanking of Morris' metal ladle clanging against the pot as he covered another pan of enchiladas with sauce.

He'd been happy when he was in his mother's kitchen, but here, Everett was positively euphoric.

The idea of going back to the loneliness of his own café, where he was the only one cooking, seemed unthinkable now that Everett knew he could have this.

It was time to close Java Joe's. He'd find a spot in someone else's kitchen, where he could enjoy being on a team while learning the rest of what he needed to know before opening his own successful restaurant. Bernardo would probably write him a letter of recommendation. And maybe Morris, too.

What if he hunted for a position in Nashville? Instead of fighting Clara for custody, he could follow her and Jimi to Tennessee, and use his off-time to focus on being the dad he'd never had himself.

He would call Clara tonight and let her know.

By the time the lunch rush was behind them, they already had three glowing reviews on CritEat.

And in the middle of the dinner rush, Sierra burst into the kitchen to announce: "I just seated Ray Joyner."

One of the world's most feared food critics was here? No wonder Evan had been freaking out when he suggested moving the opening date. What kind of PR campaign did you have to run to get Ray Fucking Joyner to show up on opening day?

"Comp him a glass of Artemis Tull and tell him we're making him one of everything," Evan said.

Then he went back to the grill and flipped a filet of halibut, as if Joyner was just another customer.

How could he be so unflappable?

Everett would be terrified to cook for one of the biggest critics in the world.

He was terrified right now, just thinking about how he could be the one to sink Tequila Mockingbird, by making a big mistake with the critic's meal.

But then he realized Evan's secret.

He wasn't overwhelmed at the thought of cooking for Ray Joyner, because he prepared every meal as if he was cooking for a world-renowned critic.

His relentless drive for consistent perfection looked exhausting from the outside. To Klair, it looked like obsession. To the junior chefs, it looked like harassment. But to Evan, it was setting a standard and holding himself to it.

By contrast, Everett had cooked every meal as if his customers were unappreciative peons who couldn't tell the difference between his egg sandwich and one from a drive-through.

And that was why Java Joe's had ultimately failed.

He turned to reach for another bucket of roasted red pepper relish and nearly collided with Morris.

"Focus up," Evan said, without looking away from the grill.

Everett muttered an apology to Morris, who clapped him on the back and whispered, "Buckle up, bitch, we've got no time for your bullshit. Ray. Fucking. Joyner."

By the time Joyner's last dish went out, Everett was back in the flow of things. He had no idea how much time had passed before Sierra returned with two thumbs up. "He said the stew was outstanding, and he wanted to know what's in the enchilada sauce."

Everyone whooped, including Evan, who didn't stop flipping shrimp for even a beat to celebrate.

The rest of the day passed in a blur, including Evan's brief interview with a journalist from *Tribeza* who'd been granted permission to take a few pictures and observe the kitchen in motion.

Everett did his best not to draw her attention as she questioned Evan, briefly turning away to grab a spare bowl of chopped cilantro when she asked where the inspiration for tonight's menu had come from.

"If you've got enough pictures, I'd be happy to talk more tomorrow," Evan curtly replied. "I've got to get back to it."

"Tomorrow," she agreed. "Ten a.m."

Everett wondered how Evan would answer that question without Everett around. Maybe he wouldn't; maybe he'd focus on the planned menu, which they'd be serving for the rest of the week, once the emergency order finally came through.

It didn't matter. He'd be on his way back to his old life by ten a.m. tomorrow.

By closing time, Sierra had brought back several dozen "compliments to the chef," and Everett thought his mother would be proud to know that so many people had enjoyed her recipes, tweaked to fit the available ingredients and Evan's preferences.

Maybe someday, once he understood the restaurant business well enough to do it right, Everett could open a little place that served her favorites. Baja Bistro.

Evan disappeared once everything had been put away for the night, but Everett understood that too. At least he got to say goodbye to his fellow station chefs.

Bernardo put one large hand on his shoulder. "All relationships have hard times, Rhett, but the best relationships are even better for the struggle. You and your brother will be fine … in time."

"I'mma miss you, bitch!" Morris wrapped his arms around Everett and lifted him an inch. Then he dropped him back to the floor and looked around the kitchen to see that Chef was already gone. "Sorry … that's some nonsense right there."

Everett agreed, but he wasn't about to complain. "It's cool. Really."

"Promise you'll hit me next time you're in Austin, even if you're not hanging with Chef?"

"If you promise to hit me if you're anywhere near Los Orillas."

Everett took one last look around the kitchen, then Everett headed for the back door.

Evan was waiting for him in the alley.

He said, "Can we talk?"

DON'T SAY ANYTHING.

It was tempting to open his mouth and start talking. But every time he'd done it before, he put his foot in his mouth. The only thing he hadn't tried was listening.

Evan lurched forward and thrust a hand into his back pocket. Everett looked and saw a baby blue box of cigarettes. *Natural American Spirit* it read on the box, just above the silhouette of a Native American puffing on the end of a peace pipe. He wondered if that packaging was still acceptable these days.

"Want one?" Evan asked.

"No thanks."

Evan nodded, put one of the American Spirits between his lips, then lit the tip and took a mighty drag.

"I didn't know you smoked," Everett said.

"I quit when I met Klair." He took another drag, exhaled in a plume. "Now I only light up when there's a day or a moment I want to I remember. My last one was when Jazz was born. The time before that was the day Señor Sushi opened."

Everett nodded.

After a long pause, Evan said, "You saved me."

"It's the least I could do."

Another long pause, then, "Klair and I talked."

"I'm sorry about—"

"Can you please just *shut up.*" Evan smiled, took a puff, then inhaled both the smoke and the silence. "Klair is right. I do need to spend more time at home."

Evan paused, and Everett wondered if he was supposed to agree, or keep his mouth shut. He opted to stay quiet.

"I wasn't happy when you first showed up on my doorstep. I thought you wanted money or something. Or that maybe you were even a con artist with a close resemblance. Maybe you looked me up online and saw the restaurant, thought you could squeeze me. Klair never agreed. She had your back from the start, always insisting that she 'just didn't get that vibe from you.' We had a fight about it. Then another fight and another after that."

And then you caught her kissing me.

"I never wanted to cause either one of you guys any trouble at all. I hate to hear that you were fighting because of me."

Evan sighed. "That wasn't your fault. We were having trouble before you showed up. But hearing her constantly defend you really made me jealous. I kept telling myself that I had nothing to worry about, but a deeper part of me was starting to believe that Klair was into you because, why not? You're like a me who wasn't being an asshole to her. At least that's how I started to see it. By the time I actually saw Klair throwing herself at you, I realized how big our problems were. And how much was my fault."

One final drag, then Evan flicked the remaining third

of his cigarette on the ground and mashed the still-burning butt with his heel.

"We're going to therapy. Klair's looking for someone now. We'll start next month. Jazz too. I didn't realize the bullying had gotten so bad."

"That's great. I've been thinking about going to therapy, too …"

"You have?" Evan asked.

"For sure." Mostly in the negative, but he'd recently changed his mind. "I've been taking Jimi and Clara for granted. For a while now. I just didn't realize it until—"

"You saw me pulling the same exact bullshit."

Everett couldn't help laughing. "Yes. That's exactly it."

"Same," Evan admitted with a nod. "It's weird how meeting you made me see myself from the outside for the first time in my life. I've spent most of my life as the center of attention, and I never really learned to share it. I'm so used to enjoying the spotlight, I didn't even know how to step outside of it when my identical twin came to surprise me on my birthday." Another shake of his head, and again the gesture felt intended for both of them. "That was a shit thing to do. You deserved a better reception."

Everett was trembling inside. "Wanna hear something really fucked up?"

"I do," Evan nodded.

"Sometimes when I was little, I actually looked forward to my brothers' bullying."

"Because at least then they were paying attention to you?" Evan guessed.

"Exactly. It was the only time they ever acknowledged my existence."

"That really is fucked up."

"Thanks." They laughed, the same sound, at the same time.

"So, the stuff you have to fix at home. How bad is it? Do you need to leave right away?" Evan asked.

"I decided to close Java Joe's. My lease is almost up, and the landlord is right to want me out of there."

"You know, if I'm working less, I'm going to need a lot more help."

Was he saying what Everett thought he was saying? "Whatever I can do."

"You would be a station chef, with a starting salary."

"That sounds … amazing." His throat was closing and his eyes were starting to sting.

"It wouldn't be fair to the others if I gave you special treatment because you're my brother."

"Of course not," Everett agreed.

He didn't want any special treatment, and he wasn't looking for an easy button. Not anymore.

Everett just wanted to find out how far he could get with his new second chance.

What to read next

Welcome to the worst day of your life.

Nils Murry has been sober for 364 days, and today, he's getting his old life back — if he can stay sober until his son's birthday party. But this day seems determined to test his resolve in every way possible. And if Nils flunks the test, he loses everything.

Get Drink Today

A Quick Favor...

If you enjoyed this book, please take a moment to write a short review on your favorite online bookstore so other readers can enjoy it, too.

Thanks so much!
Harmony Reed

About the author

Harmony Reed writes revelatory stories about what it means to live, how we can become more fully human, and how we can shed the lies we've been living by and embrace our truth. Her fiction melds the large-scale with the deeply-personal, yielding insight into the human psyche and the world we all must move through. If you enjoy authors like Michael Chabon and Jodi Picoult, movies like *Big Fish* and *Little Miss Sunshine*, or shows like *Orange is the New Black* and *This is Us*, you'll love Harmony Reed.

Also By Harmony Reed

www.ingramcontent.com/pod-product-compliance
Lightning Source LLC
Chambersburg PA
CBHW010539100726
47903CB00011B/3058